D0500314

Bold and unapologetic, Karen Shepard's *Kiss Me Someone* is inhabited by women who walk the line between various states: adolescence and adulthood, stability and uncertainty, selfishness and compassion. They navigate the obstacles that come with mixed-race identity and instabilities in social class, and they use their liminal positions to leverage power. They employ rage and tenderness and logic and sex, but for all of their rationality they're drawn to self-destructive behavior. Shepard's stories explore what we do to lessen our burdens of sadness and isolation; her characters, fiercely true to themselves, are caught between their desire to move beyond their isolation and a fear that it's exactly where they belong.

Kiss Me Someone

stories

Karen Shepard

Tin House Books
Portland, Oregon & Brooklyn, New York

Published by Tin House Books, Portland, Oregon, and Brooklyn, New York

Distributed by W. W. Norton and Company.

Library of Congress Cataloging-in-Publication Data

Names: Shepard, Karen, author.

Title: Kiss me someone : short stories / Karen Shepard.

Description: First English edition. | Portland, Oregon ; New York, New York :

 Tin House Books, 2017.

Identifiers: LCCN 2017010541 (print) | LCCN 2017013559 (ebook) | ISBN

 9781941040768 | ISBN 9781941040751 (alk. paper)

Classification: LCC PS3569.H39388 (ebook) | LCC PS3569.H39388 A6 2017 (print)

 | DDC 813/.54--dc23

LC record available at https://lccn.loc.gov/2017010541

First US Edition 2017
Interior design by Diane Chonette
www.tinhouse.com

For
Leonard and Zelda Glazer

TABLE OF CONTENTS

POPULAR GIRLS

YOU KNOW WHO WE ARE. WE'RE KAETHE AND ALINA, CJ AND Sydney. Stephanie. We're Asian or Scandinavian, white or vaguely black. We call ourselves Mayflower Madams or Tragic Mulattoes, tossing our dreadlocks, showing off our flawless skin. Our hair is blonde or brown or black. Rarely red; rarely curly. We run our fingers through it and hold it away from our faces long enough for you to see our striking eyes. When we do this, you get shivers.

It's 1984, and we sit on the benches lining our New York private school's entrance after classes are over and before we head home. They're old church pews, and we're from another world. Our canvas schoolbags mass at our feet. They're from Sweden. They come with an excess of zippers, a plastic ID tag on a small chain, and a ruler that we never use. We buy them at Chocolate Soup, the store for cool kids on Madison. We say things like, "Tenth grade is the Howard Johnson's of school life."

You can sit on these benches too, but we don't notice you. Last fall, we excised some of you from our group by taking you aside before chapel and saying, "It just isn't working out."

We see everyone who walks past, in and out of our two-hundred-year-old school. We sweep you with our eyes as if you're a landscape. We've seen everything the world has to offer, and we've dismissed it.

We lean back in the pews, our heads against the brick wall, our feet wide in front of us if we're wearing jeans. If we're wearing miniskirts, we cross our long legs and tuck one foot behind the other calf, like CJ told us she saw Anne Sexton do in a photo. We are weary. Our day was long.

Our book bags spill into the corridor in front of us, a moat. We reach into them to refold twenties into our Coach leather wallets, or to lift and then complain about that bio textbook. We mention the biology teacher's name and flutter our lashes, holding our hands over our hearts. We also discuss the theater teacher. And that one English teacher.

We have breasts. When we stretch and yawn, we arch our backs and our buttons strain. You can see bits of our Lily of France bras. We've seen the theater teacher looking at them. We're not shocked. We're not surprised. We wear them in mocha and black, dark purple and fuchsia. They're sheer and iridescent. If we're not careful, our fingernails snag on them. We don't let boys take them off. We take them off ourselves.

We listen to the tribulations of other girls' boy-friends. The boys muse about affairs. We suggest our-selves. We hold other girls' boyfriends' hands and write in our diaries: "Bingo!" We cross out the ex-girlfriends' pictures in the yearbook with a blue ballpoint pen.

We talk to senior boys on our private phones for three hours a night. We discuss girls' sexual limits. They suggest that the first time should be with an older, more experienced person. We lie under our Charlie Brown bedspreads, hug our pillows, and agree.

Some of us are virgins and some of us are not. Rumors have floated about some of us giving blow jobs in the wrestling room. Kaethe, people say, slept with Treat Williams.

Some boys we're friends with, and some we date. There's rarely any crossover. The boys we're friends with—Andy and Greg, Hunter and Miles—can join us on the pews. They sit outside the moat, on the carpeted floor, leaning forward to look at us, or leaning back on their hands. We talk about last weekend or this one. It's always a Friday in April. We consider who has passes to Studio or Xenon. An Ivy League party at Limelight. The boys hold up postcard invitations and ask if we're go-ing. We take their postcards and make no promises. We turn to each other and debate meeting at that bar, or the other one. We have fake IDs from the fake ID place on Eighth Street. They claim we go to Vassar, NYU, Columbia. We stopped going to Dublin House a year ago; that's for ninth graders. We drink on the Upper

East Side, at Dorrian's or Fitzgerald's or JG Melon. We know the managers. The bartenders give us free drinks. If we go to the West Side we go to Nanny Rose. Crayons on the table and ice-cream drinks that make our teeth ache. We pass out in the bathroom, forgotten until we're remembered and returned to the group.

We chew gum in school. On the sidewalk around the corner, out of sight of Mr. Bleakley, the upper school principal, we smoke. Virginia Slims. Lights. Some of us smoke Gitanes. Well, just CJ. If Mr. Bleakley catches us, we flirt with him until he lets us go with a warning. Stephanie touches his arm. Alina leans in close to let him smell her. We love warnings.

You can't get enough of us. You've seen girls like us every step of the way through school. We're out of your league.

We walk in the formation of migrating cranes, Stephanie at the head, Sydney and Alina on her left and right, Kaethe and CJ last. Only Kaethe cares that she's last. We haven't figured out what CJ cares about; we don't spend much time on the subject. She's Chinese, and aren't they the inscrutable ones?

Stephanie cares that she's first. She's the tallest. She was the first to wear boot-cut acid-dyed jeans. Her mother, grandmother, aunt, and great-grandmother were all ballerinas. She danced for the New York City Ballet. She was in *The Nutcracker* when she was eight. She gave it up at thirteen. Her mom was pissed. Stephanie says she's going to be a fashion designer. In her Swedish book bag she carries an artist's sketchbook and colored pencils. Sometimes she just peels back the cover of her book and starts working on her fall line. She designs her company logo. She says with a sweep of her arm that when we grow up, she'll dress us all. Her father lives in a castle. Her grandmother was the queen of Holland or something like that.

We live on Eighty-Ninth and Park, and Sixty-Sixth off Fifth, and Sutton Place in penthouses and duplexes and town houses. CJ lives in SoHo where there is a portrait of her done by someone famous. We roller-skate in parquet hallways and throw water balloons from roof gardens tended by Japanese men whose names we don't know. We get stoned in walk-in closets organized by color and in guest rooms we've never seen used. We make our Sasson jeans fit just right by putting them on and soaking in tubs filled with warm water in mirrored bathrooms.

To school, we wear sweater vests from Benetton in maroon and forest green and bright pink over men's white T-shirts. Sometimes a bandana around our necks. Our socks match our vests. We wear wool side-zip tapered-ankle trousers in yellow and purple and red from Fiorucci, or dyed painters' pants from Reminiscence. We wear boys' black penny loafers with dimes in them, or black suede booties that make us look like we're from Sherwood Forest. We wear watches with black metal bands that are slightly oversized and slide up and down our forearms like bracelets.

We wear some makeup—Sydney wears the most; she was the first to use lip liner—but we're naturally radiant without it. Men look at us when we walk by. Men with jobs and wives and children not much younger than us.

On weekends our clothes get shorter and tighter. Lycra is involved. For fancy occasions, Ungaro, Versace, Armani, or small French designers that only the French have heard of. Those of us who can't quite afford to keep buying Versace dry-clean the outfits and return them. CJ wears vintage. Her Bond Villain outfits, she calls them.

There's a certain Cartier ring. A must according to Stephanie, whose father buys only from Cartier. Three interlocking bands of three different kinds of gold: yellow, white, and pink. Its name is the name of our school, and we take that as a sign. Stephanie says a lot of knock-offs are on the market. Stephanie says she can tell the difference. Some of us tuck our hands under our thighs.

Our rooms are designed by architects and interior decorators famous for their work on small museums and boutique hotels. Our rooms are multileveled and carpeted with custom-made circular beds—an extra one for sleepovers. Or they are sunken, with marquetry wood floors designed to look like Persian rugs. We have first-generation big-screen TVs and phones in the shape of something else: Mickey Mouse, Elvis, a red Mercedes 280SL. We have cordless stereos the color of steel, Cy Twombly throw pillows, and Steiff stuffed animals: horses and goats and elephants. We have doll collections our fathers add to every time they go to a foreign country, and add-a-pearl necklaces begun by our mothers on our first birthdays. Our glass animal collections we add to ourselves. Our walls are decorated with Rolling Stones and Police posters and the *New Yorker* cover with New York as the center of the world. If our parents are art collectors we have child-appropriate Jim Dine prints of hearts or red robes.

Our parents are the presidents of department stores, interior decorators, film directors, investment bankers, psychiatrists, royalty, real estate developers. Housewives, board volunteers, fundraisers, art collectors, alcoholics, adulterers. Angry, sad, and distant. Or they're Legal Aid lawyers, doctors in Harlem clinics, cancer researchers, cooperative-nursery-school directors. Empathetic, energetic, and loving. They mystify and enrage and enthrall us. Stimulate and bewilder us, frustrate and entertain us. Very rarely, they surprise us. Mostly they bore us. We evade them, slipping around corners like cats, not wanting to confront their gifts and legacies. We tell each other they don't know the real us. We worry that even they can see through us.

We tell them we're going to one another's houses for sleepovers, and they know we're lying but let us go anyway. Have a good time, they say. Don't stay up too late. Okay, we say. We love you, we say. And we do.

This Friday in April 1984, we are on our way to the Ivy League Limelight party when a limo pulls up alongside us on Park Avenue. Boys are in the limo. Not boys we're friends with. The kind of boys we could date. They're older. Older than college. Old enough for jobs. But we're not curious about what they do. They're drinking champagne. They're wearing open-collared shirts in white and blue and lime green to show off their tans. They speak with accents. They're named Gilles and Pablo and Antoine.

Only three of them, but who cares? the five of us think, stepping gracefully into their long black car, bending so they can see whatever it is they want. *I will be one of the three*, each of us thinks. I will be one of the three they choose, nosing ahead of the other girls like horses at the wire.

We offer our hands, and they take them, but only to pull us to them, to kiss us on both cheeks. They keep their lips to our faces longer than they should.

The boys mix us Kir Royales and we giggle at the bubbles the cubes of sugar make. They introduce us to the chauffeur, a young black man to whom we give our small, kind smiles. CJ thinks he's hot. The boys ask where such a beautiful pack of women could be going on such a beautiful night, and we don't reveal how thrilled we are at being called women. We pull the postcard invitations from our sequined evening bags. They read and frown and say, *S'il vous plait*, and rip our postcards into pieces, and we laugh and open the windows for them and watch the pieces fly away.

We're not on Park Avenue anymore, and we ask them to close the window. And Gilles takes Sydney's hand and kisses her palm and the rest of us are jealous. Welcome, these men say. Welcome.

They take us to the new club. They're on the list. They know the bouncer. So do we, of course, from another club, another time. They hold their hands to the smalls of our backs, ushering us past the people who have to wait. The club is called Area; it has a long entrance tunnel lined with the equivalent of shop windows. Tonight is Red Night, and all the window tableaux have something to do with red. Real people stand in the windows. Beautiful women with bored, superior faces. Alina says she recognizes one of them from a *Seventeen* shoot she did a few months ago. Antoine pulls her dark hair back to get a better look and says he thought he'd recognized her. The rest of us silently swear to give up another two meals a week, to eat raw fruit and vegetables, to get back to 100 or at the very most 105.

But we don't like the windows. There's something about them. We walk quickly to get past them into the club, where it's dark and hot and too loud to think.

We dance to Billy Idol and Modern English, "Mony Mony" and "I Melt with You" and "I Love Rock 'n' Roll" and extended dance versions of "Every Little Thing She Does Is Magic," and Blondie's "Rapture," and anything by the Cars.

We like the dance floor. We dance in groups, letting the boys in, closing them out. Dancing is not about the boys. It's a performance of us, the group of us. Our energy, our happiness. The good things that happen when we come together. We hold our arms above our heads. We swivel our hips. We flip our hair as if we're out of control.

We point to one another and smile. Look at you, we're saying. Look at you. We're happy to be together, part of something and not alone, and we celebrate that out loud.

Off the dance floor are the bar and the bathroom. At the bar we drink Tanqueray and tonics or Melon Balls or Cape Codders, and thwart unwanted advances by putting our arms around each other and standing tall. "Sorry," we say. "We're together." If the guy hangs around, we ignore him and drop our voices to say, "What a dork," "What a loser." CJ likes more theatrical dialogue; sometimes being Chinese gives her the right: "You are so hot," she'll whisper in Kaethe's ear. "I want to lick you all over." Certain guys go for CJ.

In the bathroom, we pee quickly, and stand at the mirror in a row, brushing and talking and dabbing and talking. If we do cocaine in one of the stalls we go in by twos, using that cool little bullet of CJ's that's clear acrylic and looks like it should be in the design section of MoMA. We compare this week's to last's, reflecting on the sordidness of our dealers. Our dealers are not real dealers. They're private-school boys whom real dealers use to get to us. We also do speed. CJ does shrooms. Occasionally, we get stoned, but we agree that we were pretty much over the pot thing by the end of seventh grade. We're tenth graders. It's all about getting through the whole thing as fast as possible. Who wants to go through tenth grade in real time?

CJ collapses on the red velvet divan in the ladies' room. "Hey," she says. "I don't feel so good."

We gather round. Her skin is pale, but her skin is always pale. She has rings under her eyes. Her eyes freak us out. They're shiny, too shiny to be a sign of anything good.

She holds her head. She lists to the left. She hangs her head between her knees. She lifts it.

"You're crying," we say, pointing.

"I am?" she says, reaching to her face.

Sydney takes over. Sydney says she's going to be a doctor. Sydney's father is a heart surgeon. She kneels by CJ and feels for a pulse. She looks closely at CJ's face. She stands up and turns to us. "She's really cold," Sydney says. We nod.

The door opens. It's Pablo, wanting to know what's up. We fill him in. He comes over to the divan and we glance around, disconcerted. A boy in the girls' bathroom.

He says she probably ate or drank something bad. We nod. He'll take her back to their place and keep an eye on her. He has her on her feet and walking before we say anything. We follow them out. We ask CJ if this is okay. She seems to nod, and rests her head on Pablo's shoulder. He slides his hand up her back beneath her shirt, unhooks her bra with one hand and reaches around to cup her breast. It's almost gentle.

We don't walk them out. We tell her we'll hold her bag. We tell her we'll call her later. Kaethe remembers that CJ said Pablo was gross.

That leaves four of us. It's three in the morning. The crowd is thinning. Some people are heading to the late-night clubs. Others stare dumbly, trying to figure out how to get home.

We dance until the lights come on, revealing a dance floor of spilled drinks and dropped coat-check stubs, glasses holding triangles of lemon and lime. In a corner an empty condom packet. Atop one of the speakers a lipstick and compact mirror. On another a naked man with a ponytail is dancing even though the music has stopped. Very nice, we say, frowning and taking the arms of our men.

At their loft apartment—one vast rectangle—CJ is better. She's pouring upside-down margaritas into Pablo's mouth. We must, she says, holding the tequila and the triple sec to her chest, do two of these to be allowed in.

We take turns, in a black metal chair that looks like it came from Rent-A-Center, tilting our heads back for CJ to pour. Alina gags on her first and spits it all over Antoine. We laugh. Stephanie is a pro. Sydney and Gilles are already on the couch. He accordions her miniskirt and rubs the skin beneath the elastic of her underwear.

We notice the three beds. There are five of us, three of them. With these boys, there will be consecutive sex or two-on-ones or more-than-two-on-ones. Whatever happens will be performed in front of the group. We ask ourselves whether we can actually do this; we imagine how we'll step out of our clothes gracefully. We're uneasy. Nothing about this whole thing will be graceful. No one is leaving.

It's five in the morning by now. In our homes our parents who love us are still sleeping. Our younger brothers and sisters, who think we're way cool but who tease us mercilessly, have kicked off their covers and are murmuring in their dreams. Our dogs have their tails curled over their twitching noses; our cats are prowling the kitchens. Our goldfish named Snoopy and Linus are floating in their bowls. And there we are, in our beds too. Wearing our all-cotton pajamas, sleeping the sleep of the innocent, the young, the entitled. Our arms are flung above our heads; our legs are hanging uncovered off the side of the bed. It doesn't matter. There we are. So here in this apartment with three men whose last names we don't know, it doesn't matter what happens. We're loved. We're protected. Do with us what you dare. Do with us what you can.

FIRE HORSE

1.

PROTECT YOURSELF, MY GRANDMOTHER TOLD ME. ALWAYS.

She told me someday my mother would leave me for the latest boyfriend. We were in Chengdu, Szechuan. It was August of 1975. I was nine years old and there against my father's wishes. I didn't really want to be there either. I would've rather been spending the summer with my father and half brother watching unsupervised TV and eating pretzels and ice cream. But I wasn't saying anything to either of my parents. It was something, being the object of all that tension between them.

Weeks before we left New York, my grandmother had told me over the phone from her apartment in Paris that it was only a matter of time before my mother would lose interest in me, now that I was grown up.

Grown up? I thought. And I hadn't known I'd *had* her interest to lose. My brother always said my mother was impossible to read. Who could tell what was going on in that alien mind of hers?

The year before, on one of her visits, my grandmother had asked if my mother wanted to find her mother.

My mother looked unsurprised by the question. That was the first I'd heard she was adopted. I hadn't done that well at getting more information since.

One hundred seven in the shade, the grown-ups kept saying. All around us contraptions designed to fight the Szechuan heat: my mother, it turned out, had been born in a hot, damp place. Industrial-sized fans blew over two-foot-square blocks of ice in metal tubs in our hotel room. The colder air chilled our ankles if we stood close enough. Thin mats of rice straw over the padded cotton coverlets on our beds were supposed to cool our sleep. They left me sticky, marked with impressions on the backs of my legs and the side of my face. We waved pleated paper fans with scenes of lotus flowers and goldfish ponds and terraced mountains in front of our flushed faces, our tired eyes.

Parts of me could be cooled, but never at once and never all together. The heat of interior China got un-der my fingernails, onto the nape of my neck, and be-neath the shade of my hair. I refused to give in to my grandmother and wear my hair up in the pigtails of my Chinese counterparts: high above the ears and tied with red glossy bows that matched the Red Guard scarves around their necks. So that their black bundled hair bounced and shook obediently.

See, my grandmother would tell me, *they* won't get prickly heat. They're smarter than American children.

I wore my hair down with plastic headbands. Yes, I would answer, just short of polite. I see.

My all-American father always called her Empress Dowager. Dragon Lady.

He called her fourth and longest-lasting husband Broken Man and Doormat.

My brother never called either of them anything.

My full-Chinese mother had called her Mommy, then Mother, then, finally, Margaret, when she discovered that "Mother" wasn't biologically accurate. This sea change had come about when my mother was twenty-one and a family friend had asked whether she ever heard from her mother. Yes, my mother answered, just last week. No, the family friend had said, meaning no harm. Your *real* mother.

I'd finally gotten that part of the story a few months before the trip to China.

I called her Grandma anyway, seduced by the notions of family, tradition, three generations in stair-step order. I stared at her whenever I got the chance. I liked her thick, chopped hair in which she was always losing her hands. She had supple fingers that sliced the air, accompanying her stresses. She could silence a room with those hands. I admired that. Her part-Asian, part-European face was the closest thing the family had to offer to my own half-and-half face. Like me, I thought: all mixed up. I was maudlin at times.

What are you, Ori-Yenta? my father asked on our last night together before I left for China. Chewish? my brother offered. They were trying to get me to say I didn't want to go.

I stood on my father's bed and with my hand sliced a line down the center of me. "Here is Mom," I said. "Here is you."

"And where am I?" my brother wanted to know.

In Chengdu in August of 1975, I was having trouble believing that any part of me came from a place like this. I missed cold glasses of cold milk. I missed rolls and bagels. Air-conditioned movie theaters and bedrooms. I wanted my mother to miss the same things.

Ai ya, the Chinese adults would wail, holding me by my shoulders, she doesn't look Chinese. So tall. Such wavy hair. Those feet.

My feet were my father's. Long and skinny, he always said, wrapping his hands around my ankles.

I look, I finally answered them, glancing over at my mother, like my father.

My father and mother had both managed to be orphans with living parents. My father's father died in the flu epidemic when my father was two, and my mother's father in the war when my mother was the same age.

My father's mother had put him in a Philadelphia orphanage, and my mother's mother had sold her to the richer and more educated and barren woman I knew as Grandma. My father had moved out of *our* apartment when I was three. A break in the pattern. Sometimes it pleased me to imagine that this made me an orphan, but of course it didn't.

At two, my mother had been the right age: old enough to be finished nursing and young enough not to know what she was leaving. One thousand yuan, the story went, for a round-faced ringwormed girl baby. But the story—my grandmother's story—changed. She was a writer with five volumes of memoirs, so sometimes it wasn't a peasant family but a middle-class family with just one too many girls. Sometimes my mother was my grandfather's illegitimate child, and my grandmother was the martyr. I heard my mother tell her once, finally, that she'd stopped wondering which version to believe.

The way I imagined it my grandmother paid for her and brought her home and sat on the bed with her, touching her glossy hair. She read to her. I liked to imagine my war baby mother in my grandmother's lap, turning her face to the sky and saying *boom*, and letting my grandmother know what, at the age of two, she had already been taught would come from the sky.

. . .

My grandmother ate spicy food. Chili peppers straight off the stalk. She kept two or three plants in her apartment in Paris for that purpose. I had seen her walk by and pop red, yellow, or orange tear-shaped chilies into her mouth. I'd waited for her eyes to water, her fingers to pinch her nose, her mouth to form a cooling *oh*. Instead, she chewed, she swallowed, she curled her tongue up onto her lip. She ate another.

I'd been impressed, and I still was. I wanted to be able to hold that kind of heat inside me.

On the plane, my mother had been more soggy with sentiment than I expected, touched with herself for dragging her daughter back to the site of her childhood unhappiness. She got reminiscent. She got intimate, and ready to open up. By hour thirteen of the flight, I was hair-pullingly bored with her attempts at connection and let her know it. She continued to reminisce and I played hangman. Trying to scare up a little narrative interest, she strayed into areas I didn't know about. She brought up my brother. She dropped some details.

Hating myself, I had to ask anyway. How did *she* know? He was a half brother, my father's from a first marriage. When did *they* spend any real time together?

She looked away, like someone on a soap miming *If you only knew*.

"*What?*" I asked, annoyed. She was excited. She was Close to Something.

Didn't I know? she asked, lowering her voice, as if the stewardess cared. Hadn't she ever told me that he'd been a little in love with her?

This was what life with my mother was like.

"My *brother*. My brother was in love with *you*," I said, once I recovered.

She gave me a look.

"You just *guessed*?" I said.

"I wouldn't guess a thing like that," she said, irritated that I'd think so.

Which led to unpleasant thoughts or images. She must have seen some of them on my nine-year-old face.

"We never *did* anything, silly," she said.

"He told you he liked you? You never did anything?" I asked. The woman in the seat in front of us turned around. I had seven hours of flight still to go.

"You're going to make it something it wasn't," she said.

I cried intermittently the first four days after landing. My grandmother assumed I was having a psychotic episode. She gave me special tea and the special tea gave me diarrhea. The diarrhea made me weepier. Finally my mother in exasperation called over from her pallet in the middle of the night that she'd only been *kidding*, for God's sake; he hadn't said or done anything. What was wrong with me?

Nothing was wrong with me, I thought, lying there, fixing my eyes on her outline in the dark. I didn't need the light to see how beautiful she was. Her beauty was the kind that made people who wanted to hate her reconsider. Nothing was going to be wrong with me again.

The next day, as far as anyone could tell, I was fine.

"Don't ask me what *that* was all about," my grandmother said, after having satisfied herself that it was over.

In Szechuan, where food wasn't spicy but just food, they had to remove the pepper for me. In honor of our visit, the local branch of the US-China Peoples Friendship Association organized a dinner. My grandmother's memoirs and books on China had made her a celebrated link between East and West, and these people, my grandmother whispered to my mother on our way down to dinner, might be able to help her in her search.

On an easeled blackboard by the door to the dining room someone had written "We Welcome You Home" with wide strokes of multicolored chalk. Underneath the words, a drawing of my grandmother's latest book, pages ruffling in unseen wind.

Why, I had once asked her in a Second Avenue restaurant, if she loved China so much, didn't she live there.

Because, she answered, looking at me over the collar of her favorite mink coat, she could do more for China by living in the West.

Oh, I said, young and stupid.

Though the chef at the dinner had used all seven of the traditional Szechuan flavors in our honor, I could eat only sweet, salty, and nutty. At first, no one even made me try the hot of the red chili and hot bean paste, the fragrant of the garlic and ginger, the sour of the vinegar, or even the bitter of mild green onions and leeks.

Platters circled on the lazy Susan holding chicken fashioned back into the shape of a rooster with a radish as a crown, or beef topped with green onions with a teaspoonful of white pepper hidden under the pile, or China Sea scallops bathed in vinegar, garlic, ginger, and hot bean paste.

"*Ai ya*," my grandmother complained to everyone. "*Ai ya*," she wailed. Everyone was always wailing. "Her mouth is like a baby's," she said. "*I* gave her mother a Chinese mouth. Why her mother couldn't do the same, I'll never know."

My mother began to say something, but didn't, then turned to me and told me to put some more food on my plate.

"Eat," she whispered. "Don't ask for special treatment." She spooned some of the scallops onto my plate.

"*Wo zi ze lai*," I whispered back. It was one of the only things I knew how to say: I can help myself.

"Finish it," she said, and tapped the rim of my bowl with her chopsticks without looking at me.

I cradled the bowl and used my chopsticks to shovel in the scallops. I cleaned the corners of my mouth.

"Cut it out," she whispered.

"What?" I asked, my mouth still full.

"You know what," she said, turning to someone else.

Later, I knelt on the bathroom tiles and threw up into the toilet. She stood behind me and touched me between my shoulder blades, and I flinched her hand away. She gathered my hair from my face. I told her it was her fault. I told her she should've just left me at home. What was I doing here anyway? I missed my father. Which wasn't true; I knew what a month with my father could be like. She did too. She'd divorced him. I missed my brother; that *was* true. There wasn't anything I could do about it, though, and it wasn't as though he missed me.

Later, in bed, I told her I thought it was that sauce she had made me eat, but I secretly thought it was what she'd said about my brother.

She reminded me from her mat that the Chinese said that a cook could pour that sauce over rocks and hungry people would eat them happily.

I asked in response just when she had found out she was adopted.

She came over to sit on the side of my twin bed and told me what she knew. Then when I didn't respond she said she was glad she had spent so many years not talk-ing to her mother, and she was glad she'd started calling her Margaret. She was glad she'd gotten to give up on my grandmother first.

I told her that was sad. Like at school when you told someone you didn't think you could be friends and that person said it was okay because they'd already stopped liking you.

When I saw her face, I added that I was sad that she had been left by two mothers.

And to make her feel better, I told her I was the luckiest. I hadn't been left at all. And what she was doing to Grandma was right. Getting up from my bed, reaching down to stroke my cheek, she agreed that, yes, I was the lucky one. And afterward, lying there, listening to her cry in the bathroom, I marveled at how easy it was to do or undo enormous damage. I told myself to remember this.

The night of the Friendship Association dinner, my grandmother paid a tailor to stay up and make a surprise for me. In the morning, she had the guides cancel the tour of the silkworm factory, and took us to a windowless shop where a man in thick glasses sat on a three-legged stool. I looked at the army green material in his lap. This was the surprise?

My grandmother strode around offering comments that I imagined were compliments on his workplace, its tidiness.

My mother leaned down. The tailor had been up all night making this for me. Remember that, she said.

It was a Red Guard uniform with knee-length shorts, a jacket with button-down flap pockets, a canvas belt with a brass buckle. A matching cap with a slick red plastic star sewn to the front. The red scarf I had seen around the necks of all the other children.

They'd made me feel spoiled and petty. They'd met us at the doors of middle schools, children's centers, after-school gymnasiums and presented me with bouquets of plastic flowers. They'd stood up straight at the front of classrooms and recited English poetry. I was continually presented with children who had earned their nicknames—Brother Strength, Sister Fierce, Little Pride—by performing some feat beyond adult capabilities.

I'd already been told about the six-year-old who painted traditional landscapes better than the old masters, the eight-year-old who jumped into a raging river to save his mother, the nine-year-old who retraced the path of the Long March in honor of Chairman Mao and the Party. Children to live up to. A task at which, my grandmother understood, I would never succeed but should attempt anyway.

Photos were taken. The tailor and me. Me between my mother and grandmother. Me by myself.

My grandmother said that was the one we would send my father.

I admired her for her cruelty.

I imagined my brother seeing it. I imagined what my father would say: Jesus Christ. She's only *half* Chinese for Chrissake. Where the hell am I in this picture?

In Chinese, I was called *Jiu Ru*. I was taught to put my name into a context. *Jiu*: nine, as in seven, eight, nine. *Ru*: the *ru* in *ru yi*, pieces of imperial jade; the *ru* used to make the word *if*. In English: desires. Nine Desires. The nine most wished-for attributes of a girl child. Things like purity. I didn't learn them all. Wit and prudence. Since we'd arrived, my grandmother and my mother used only that name. It always took a moment to remember whom they were calling.

On the plane, before the news flash about my brother, my mother had given me an astrology book. In the Chinese zodiac, I was a Horse. I was pleased. What nine-year-old girl wouldn't like being a Horse?

It was a perfect sign for me, my mother and grandmother agreed.

I read that Horses had the ability to sway a crowd and were creatures of changing moods, hot-blooded, hotheaded, impatient. That anyone who suffered one of their rages would never feel quite the same again. They were more cunning than intelligent, and they knew it. Above all, Horses were selfish: they would trample anyone blocking their way without remorse. Their ambition was all-consuming, especially in the area of love. Horses would give up everything for love.

I looked over at my mother. I was flattered about the passionate part and appalled at the rest. I kept reading.

I'd been born in the year of the Fire Horse, which occurs only once every sixty years. The Fire Horse had the same characteristics as the Horse, only more accentuated. Though the news wasn't all bad. The Fire Horse supposedly could be a good influence in her family— it wasn't exactly clear how—but mostly the Fire Horse would make trouble in the home she was born in and the one she would build. Some women in fact resorted to abortion rather than allowing themselves to bear a child under that sign.

It took me part of an in-flight movie to recover. When I had, I looked up my brother. He was a Snake.

Wise and determined. Hated to fail. Shocking. I tapped my mother's arm and asked what her sign was.

Dragon. I looked it up in my book.

Of course, the Dragon turned out to be admirable. The only mythological animal among the twelve, exotic and revered. Dragons were sought out. Dragons had fertile imaginations. They were the causes of chaos and were surrounded by others who worried for them, who picked up the pieces. I did some birthday calculations: my grandmother, my father, my mother—all Dragons.

When I was an infant, my grandmother supposedly always wanted me in her lap. In most early photos that's where I'm sitting. Usually her hands are out of focus, waving a cigarette. My mother told me that sometimes my grandmother would forget I was there and get up. I told my mother that this explained my expression in the photos. I also wanted to know: Did she ever catch me when I was tumbling to the floor?

During our second week in Chengdu, my mother found an old woman who said of course she remembered the little girl baby. She had made my mother's first pair of pants and shoes.

I had seen those shoes. They sat on my mother's bookshelves next to antique snuff bottles and small porcelain boxes. I wasn't allowed to touch. Those sorts of things I was drawn to whenever my mother went out of the apartment. The day before we left for China, I opened boxes, cracked book spines, tried on earrings. I uncapped bottles, held them up to the light, tried to see through them. I left things out of place.

I left the shoes on the floor. They were black cotton slip-ons. The soles were layers of white cotton sewn together with black thread. My mother had stuffed them with little wads of newspaper that had gone yellow long ago. I pulled the newspaper out, replacing it with my fingers, feeling the grainy, oily scratchiness of the cloth's underside. I saw my grandmother coaxing my mother's baby foot into this shoe for the first time. She must have held the lower leg just so, wiggling the shoe to get it to slip up and over the small heel. Then I replaced the newspaper as if my mother wouldn't notice and tiptoed out of the room as if she were already home.

This old woman in Chengdu went on about the shoes at a round concrete table beneath a banyan tree. There was no breeze. Mosquitoes circled my ankles.

Everyone watched and listened. No one translated. My mother mimicked the woman's movements as if anything less than synchronicity would mean missed information and lost meaning.

"Mom," I whispered finally. "What? What's she saying?"

My mother continued staring, held her hand out, palm down, and told me to hush a minute. Just wait.

I had never seized my mother's attention like that. I sat back in my chair and stopped imagining what the woman could be saying. I stopped wishing for her to say what I thought my mother wanted to hear. I started wishing the search would just be over whether my mother found what she was looking for or not.

When the old woman took a break to reach for her tea, my mother said, "She's telling me about the shoes. The ones we have at home."

I told her I was hot. I had a stomachache. I wanted to go home.

She said if I was hot, if I had a stomachache, I should go back to the car and lie down. She couldn't do anything about going home right now.

Asking was not the way to get things from my mother.

When my mother had left Paris to go to college, my grandmother had thrown away everything she left behind. Stuffed animals, handmade dolls with suitcases full of outfits, books. Photographs. Drawings of the houses they had lived in, the pets they had had. Diaries. Notebooks.

My mother coming home for the holidays, standing in the doorway to what used to be her room, and taking breaths before asking why; my grandmother looking into the neater, tidier room and telling her she was far too old for all that stuff, before she moved on down the hallway: this, knowing them, was how it must have gone.

The morning after the shoe lady, I looked for my mother. I hadn't slept well. My stomach had hurt, and I spent most of the night sitting up in bed hugging a pillow, glancing over to see if I was waking her.

I walked down the hallway to my grandmother's suite. Her status had earned us the privilege of staying in the guesthouse for dignitaries. We were the only visitors.

The corridor was still and hot. Under my footsteps, I crushed the pale green carpet that displayed scenes from Chairman Mao's life. It had been handmade in less than a week by an entire village to celebrate his last birthday. It was over fifty feet long. I walked over a round-faced baby holding on to the chairman's enormous ring finger.

My mother used to tell me that it was too hard to walk on New York sidewalks while holding hands.

We could try, I would say.

But in the winter she wanted to keep her hands in her pockets, and in the summer, it was too hot. She would wipe her brow as proof.

Just fingers, I would suggest, linking my pinkie with hers, and we would walk like that until she unhooked herself and I pretended to have forgotten what I wanted in the first place.

At my grandmother's room, the double doors were ajar. I stopped, looked through the space between door and door frame, and listened.

My grandmother said to my mother that her real mother probably didn't even want to see her. That was a distinct possibility.

"More than a possibility," my grandmother said. "Probability. She did give you up. Remember?"

It was hard to tell how much damage she was doing. I could see my mother light a cigarette. I had never seen her smoke. She seemed to know how to do it. My grandmother meanwhile was peeling a peach. One of those white, over-sized peaches that I hadn't known existed until I went to China. Their flesh was creamy, a translucent white. Their juices ran like water being squeezed from a bath sponge. We ate them, sticky, wet, and sweet, as if surrendering to the heat.

"I didn't ask for this search," my mother said.

My grandmother peeled her peach. She laid each strip of skin to the side of a saucer that was collecting the juice and wiped her hands clean with a dampened towel and said something in Chinese.

My mother didn't answer.

"But you wanted it," my grandmother said, and licked her fingertips.

To get anything from my mother, you had to make her believe the giving was her idea. You had to make her believe you didn't really want it, that it hadn't occurred to you to ask.

To get my ears pierced I told her that one day I wanted to look like her, but that probably I never would because, you know, my father had said he would never let me get my ears pierced.

He has nothing to do with it, my mother answered. I could tell him she said so.

When the latest boyfriend had moved into the apartment, I would call out from my bedroom down the hall.

Mom, I have a stomachache. Mom, Come here. Just for a minute. It really hurts.

Rub it, she would call back. Get a glass of milk. Lie on your side. Hug a pillow.

I would wait long enough for it to seem like I might have tried those things, and then would walk quietly down the hall, hugging myself with crossed arms for the last few steps. Mom, I would say, outside of her room, spying. It really hurts.

Had I done all the things she suggested, she wanted to know.

Yes. Nothing worked. It hurt. Right here. In my side.

Come in, she might say. Let me see.

And I would push open the door, still hugging myself, and walk to the bed. Only the bedside light would be on, and the boyfriend would roll up off the bed and go to the bathroom, or down the hall, or somewhere, and I would kneel on the bed and lie next to her, my head on her pillow, to show her where it hurt.

Here? she would say, touching my side. Here?

And I would shake my head a few times before nodding yes. And I would lie there feeling my mother's hand through my cotton nightgown, forgetting to listen for his steps in the hallway, remembering to keep my eyes closed.

They were still talking. I was still in the hall. I pushed open the double doors and walked in. "I couldn't find you," I said.

My grandmother finished her peach and wiped her hands one final time with the towel. "Here," she said. "She's here, with me."

My mother turned back to my grandmother and put out her cigarette. "This was your idea," she said. "It was you who told me this would be easy. If you're changing your mind now, don't worry. It wouldn't be the first time, would it?"

"Mom," I said, going over to her, "my stomach hurts."

She told me I should've stayed in bed. My grandmother told me I was getting to be quite the invalid. My mother added she would get me some soda.

"What's this about stomachaches," my grandmother said when my mother left the room. "First it was your head. Then, your eyes. Now, your stomach. What to do? We'll have to take you to the hospital and get you a good acupuncture treatment. Douse you with Chinese medicine—ginseng and deer antlers, tadpoles and snake eggs."

I sat in the chair my mother had just left and listened.

She pointed out the differences between me and my Chinese peers. They had a stronger will, did I know that? They knew how to will away illness. I knew nothing of true suffering.

I rolled my eyes, but what she was saying was true.

How would I ever make anything of myself? she wanted to know. I had no discipline. I should walk in mud for eight hours. Carry water to my starving family.

I asked if *she* had ever walked in mud. If *she* had ever carried water to her starving family.

She was still. I looked away. I felt her leaning toward me.

"Another thing," she said quietly. "You have no sense of family. You have no sense at all of respect."

I held my stomach with one hand, the back of my neck with the other.

See, she told me, lifting my hair. Prickly heat. The sign of the weak.

She reached over for the scissors on the desk. She held the hair she had and hacked her way through like someone clearing trails.

I squeezed my eyes shut.

"I should've known *you* would cry," she said.

I can tell Dad, I thought. *I can tell my brother.*

Behind me I heard my mother come back in the room—*I tried to help you*, I thought, almost convincing myself.

"Hold still," my grandmother said, as much to my mother as to me.

My mother said nothing.

I want her to stop, I thought. I clamped my hands to my head. My grandmother cut around them.

No, I thought, *I want to be able to* make *her stop.*

So I told my mother that her real mother probably didn't want to see her. That was a distinct possibility. And the room sharpened and cooled. And the scissors stopped.

2.

BACK HOME, YEARS LATER, I NOT ONLY COUNTED THE NUMBER of times my brother left me, I categorized them in a journal. *Accidental* meant couldn't be helped. *Voluntary* meant the ones for which I held him responsible. In that category I stuck forgotten meetings, blown-off movie dates, family gatherings. Parties with friends to which I was supposed to have been invited. Lovers. Marriages. Weddings. Wives.

He was thirteen years older. He was with his mother full-time, but some weekends and most summers he came to stay with our father and me. Our father traveled a lot.

My brother's first wife left him when he was twenty-eight. He'd been married for two years. The rest of the family wanted to know what happened.

I wanted to know too; I just didn't want to have to ask. I waited for him to volunteer, and when he didn't, that was all right, too. I just made sure I was around for whatever happened next.

Three years after his divorce, my brother had more bad news. He told me over Christmas break. I was a senior at a private school. I was wearing a plaid skirt rolled at the waist with fishnet stockings and black riding boots. We were in his favorite restaurant, at one of nine tables. He'd taken his first wife here for special occasions. This was where he'd asked her to marry him. The table in the bay window apparently.

The new girlfriend was tall, he said. She was beautiful. She was closer to my age than his. She had a little girl.

Instant family, I told him. From the back of the restaurant, an electric blender racketed. Margaritas.

He looked to the bar. "It's just living together," he said. "It's not like marriage."

He hadn't lived with anyone since the first wife left, though I had stayed with him for two days. "She was in and out," he could've said about my visit. "I can't even remember what we did." That was what I'd told my mother, in fact, when she'd asked, with an odd focus in her voice, how the visit had gone. I told her I couldn't remember. Apparently neither could he. He never talked about it again.

And with how many girls was that the case? My brother finished and moving on, and them still hanging on, dreamy and stupid?

So sitting there at his first wife's favorite restaurant, I wasn't saying boo.

He wiped the salt off his glass with his index finger. What if he was making a big mistake? he wanted to know.

Around us people gestured with forks, drinking and talking. It was like a movie. I could feel the slow zoom.

"What if you are?" I said back.

He looked at my hairline.

"I want to go away with you," he said. "Let's escape right here in the city. Two nights of incognito."

I kept a fixed look on my face, but I wasn't really breathing.

We could get a hotel room. Somewhere fancy. His eyes moved left to right across my face. He knew a place.

I bet, I thought. He took a girlfriend to an abortion clinic once and the nurses greeted him by name, like Norm in *Cheers*. He told me this. But my insides were doing unsurprising and amazing things, and I flashed on a vacation when I'd gone swimming with dolphins, their gray muscled bodies skimming by with nothing to spare.

I had to decide in the next few days, I was informed. The new girlfriend was on a snowboarding vacation and was going to be back on Monday. It was Thursday.

He took a bite of his curry. I put my dessert fork on top of my dinner fork.

"Why?" I finally asked. "Why this now?"

He didn't smile or tell me he was kidding. He ran his hands through his hair. He hadn't taken his eyes off me.

"Because," he said.

"That's not an answer," I said.

"Then *just* because," he said.

And it was left at that. Because I had nothing to add.

...

My brother wasn't bringing up sex with me out of the blue. The second of those two nights I'd stayed over when I was fifteen and his first wife had just left him, we'd had wine and danced in the dining room with the lights out. He took me by the back of my neck. We stopped. We sank to the floor, breathing hard, sweating in the darkness. I opened my shirt. I was cross-legged on the rough carpet. I combed my hands through his hair the way I'd seen him do it himself. I pushed it back, kept my hands buried in it, and brought his mouth to my breast. I thought of my mother.

I waited for his mouth to close around me. I waited for the rest of it. I waited for the cue to arch my back, to let my mouth give myself away. I waited for the last bit of proof that I'd been right all along. That we had known.

But he pulled back and took me by the wrists. He held my hands down away from him, against the carpet, between our legs. He did it smoothly. And even then I knew that it wasn't making love that my brother wanted. He wasn't saying yes and he wasn't saying no, and that was him all over. He raised himself a ways up—a limbo move, he called it later—until my mouth was at the right level and unzipped himself. I did the rest. I thought while I was doing it that I was doing it for him. I'm sure he thought so, too. But I also thought it might be a way of hurting my mother. And of making something. This was eating chilies right off the plant. This was silencing a room.

...

That Saturday afternoon, he was waiting for me outside my eye doctor's office. My mother was with me. She was thrilled to see him. She strode across the street to where he was leaning against a parked car. I followed slowly, my eyes sticky and weird from whatever the doctor had done to me.

I watched them hug and kiss. They always kissed on the mouth. My brother did with everyone. My mother wanted to know what he was doing there.

"I'm here to sweep her away," he said.

In most cases, hearing him say he was there to sweep me away would have been like opening the fridge on a hot day for the cold air. In this case, the effect was weirder. Was he playing with me? I gave him a *Don't play with me* look. At the same time, I tried to communicate: *Don't say anything else about our secret.*

He pulled me to him, and I noted as always how well I fit under his arm. "We're off to have a brother/sister thing," he said. He kissed me on the cheek and let his hand fall to my rear. "Well, at least that's *my* plan," he went on. "Your daughter is waffling."

"Yes," my mother said. "She can do that."

He rested a hand on her shoulder for a beat too long. He said, "*You'd* run away with me, wouldn't you?"

She told him to stop flattering himself. She told me to call if I wasn't going to be home for dinner. Her assumptions about what could and couldn't be going on were clear. I wanted to wave my hand and make her disappear, and he knew that.

Did he think I was stupid? *Okay, fine*, I thought. *You want me? How* much *do you want me?*

"Nothing's going to happen anytime soon," I told him flatly. "This is a bad time. Maybe Tuesday, or even

Wednesday." Wednesday was supposed to be our annual Christmas shopping date. We'd scheduled it weeks ago. I was fairly certain he wouldn't remember.

He wasn't particularly discombobulated. In front of my mother, he reached out and stroked my cheek. "Wednesday's good," he said. "I can wait until Wednesday." Part of what he was selling was: *To hell with what anyone knows. To hell with what your mother knows.*

"We're going shopping anyway," he added, and I was reminded that I'd always trade being right for how he could make me feel.

My mother's expression shifted, to my satisfaction. She laughed a little. "Who knows what either of you is talking about," she said.

And I thought that in fact this *wasn't* a game I knew anything about; I didn't know the first thing about what we were up to. What *were* we talking about? What *did* we mean? But that was also thrilling. I was thrilled.

The same summer I'd given my brother a blow job, our father had rented a house by a lake. I would refuse to leave my brother's room when he wanted to change. I made him uncomfortable. I made him lower his voice. He tried various things, coaxed, bribed, and threatened until he got me to leave.

Sometimes I came back and looked. His door was always half-open. I watched him undress. He'd pull his T-shirt off the way boys do, reaching behind his head, pulling up and over. His muscles rolled with the movement. He had hair on his narrow chest, a little, around his nipples.

The three of us met for lunch the day after the new girl-friend got back. Tuesday.

"You could be full brother and sister," she said while we were still opening menus.

People told us we looked alike. Cuban, or Mexican. "But we're not," I reminded her. My brother threw me a smile.

"He's always gone out with women who look like him," she whispered to me later, when we were putting on hats and scarves, checking ourselves in the mirror by the restaurant door. She thought it was a moment of connection.

He was already out on the sidewalk waiting for us. "No danger of that here," I told her, reaching out to flick the ends of her blonde hair.

I, on the other hand, always went out with boys who looked different than me. Big blonde boys. Prep school boys. Boys with last names for first names. It may have been my way of getting a little power back.

Nazis, my father called them.

Hitler Youth was my brother's term.

They were boys who couldn't compete, couldn't keep up with me, unless I showed them how. Which was not how I felt with my brother. Somehow he'd gotten out there in the lead, and not just because of his age. How had that happened? Why had I let it happen? *Wo zi ze lai,* I thought. I can help myself.

"I could marry him," I said to my father when I was nine. We had just come back from helping my brother move into his first apartment. "If I married him, he'd have to stay."

"Sure," my father answered, deep in his favorite chair. He was absorbed in unlacing his shoes. "Marry him. Just don't have children."

Children, I thought. *That would make my mother a grandmother.*

The three of us walked down Fifty-Seventh Street after lunch, and the new girlfriend told me that Nicky really loved me.

I looked at my brother, whose face was not particularly readable.

Nicky, I thought. *Who is Nicky?*

"No," she reiterated, though I hadn't asked for reassurance, "I mean really. You mean so much to him." She said this like I was the soon-to-be-stepdaughter. "He cares about you so much."

"Is that true, Nicky?" I asked, leaning across her as we walked. "Do you care about me so much?"

His smile was a little sickly. She smiled with him. And for a terrible moment I thought they *had* been confiding in each other. Which made me think of that hotel room.

"God, too bad he's your brother," friends said when they met him.

"For Chrissake, he's your brother," my father told me when I got possessive.

"You're never going to find someone like him," my mother said, every so often.

"I met someone who's perfect for you," he said, two weeks after our dance in the dining room.

"Oh yeah?" I said, with enough judgment in my voice that he didn't call me back for weeks.

"Who?"

Once when I was fourteen we'd been in an airport together. He was married, but the wife wasn't with us. A woman in tight jeans and a suede shirt was staring at him.

He told me that she was trying to decide if I was his sister or his date. He wove our fingers together.

On the plane, that same woman came down the aisle looking for him. I feigned sleep against the window. As she passed our row, he put his hand across my lap and took my earlobe in his mouth.

We were playing odd man out and it wasn't clear who was who. We walked all the way from Fifty-Seventh to Eighty-First as a trio. He moved to the middle at Seventy-Second and walked with his arms around both of us. We were his parentheses.

We turned up Madison. The new girlfriend peeled off to more comprehensively check out some shoes in a window display. "So I'm thinking," he said in a low voice to me. "Of you."

I glanced past him to her. She was looking at her reflection in the window.

"What are you thinking about?" he asked, leaning close.

She came back and took his hand. She wanted to know what we were talking about.

He squeezed her closer and said, "We're talking about how people are wondering which one of you I'm with."

She smiled like it was an inside joke. *It* is *an inside joke*, I thought. *On any number of us.*

Before the China trip, that was the way we used to walk down Fifth Avenue: my brother in the middle, an arm around my mother and me.

I still kept a running tally of the number of times he'd touched me.

A fair number involved my toes. As a joke he pulled and tugged them until they cracked. That night in his apartment when I was fifteen, when we were still sitting in the living room, I confided my lifelong belief that they were long and ugly. Not ugly, he told me, holding them in the curve of his hands, reaching them to his mouth.

For all the kissing on the lips he did, we'd kissed only once. The first time I visited him in his own apartment. He was twenty-two. I was nine. He got me on the lips, full and square. He left no time for indecision about which cheek to turn. "Come on, come on," my mother said. "We're going to be late for dinner."

My almost-breasts once, that night when I was fifteen.

I counted my hands only when he'd taken them in his. Where? Restaurant booths. Beach blankets. City parks.

My chin once, on a picnic.

"You know," my mother reminded me when I was fifteen, the night I got back from my brief stay at his apartment. "Your brother could've been a real writer. Not just news bits and record reviews. Novels," she said. "Poetry."

At the time I was editor of the school literary magazine and the newspaper. I brought issues home and my mother marked them up with what I'd gotten wrong: small facts, street names, dates.

While she talked, I brushed my teeth with special force. I felt as if I'd turned some exciting and disgusting corner, and *this* was the kind of stuff she was telling me? Everything about me was telling *her*. Who loves who *now*?

It was Wednesday. We were on Madison again, between uptown and midtown. He wanted me to pick out something. I had the feeling I was the last person left on his list. We were in Agnès B., where everything I'd want cost too much to suggest. I was carrying my own bag and some of his packages, and things were awkward, and neither of us said anything.

We passed a bus stop billboard of a windswept model in denim.

"That's one of my favorite models," he remarked.

I hoisted one package while another slipped a little lower in my arms. "Thrilling," I told him.

He told me she was stunning and volunteered that that was the kind of thing he couldn't tell his soon-to-be but he could tell me.

"Thank God for me," I said.

He stopped and turned me to face him. He reached under all the packages and found my hips. Why wasn't *he* carrying anything? He rocked me side to side. "So?" he said. "Here I am."

He knew I knew what he meant: *You've been staring at me for however-many years like a dog without a bone. So: All right, then. Come and get it.*

. . .

After he was finished when I was fifteen I'd hugged him and we got up and I slept on the bed and he slept in the chair across from the bed, and I woke up early with the garbagemen and thought: *What did this mean? Did it mean anything? Why would I think it meant anything? How could it not mean something?*

He was awake, too, watching.

I told him I hadn't heard him moving around.

"You've been out completely," he said.

"The ultimate sign of trust," I said.

And we lay there like that. He asked what was wrong.

I told him I guessed I was just tired. He got up and trooped into the kitchen and ate some cereal.

He said it would probably be best if I went back home. And I did.

On our Christmas walk when I didn't answer and he let go of my hips, and we started walking again, he told me he was getting married.

So much for just living together. It felt like one of his smooth *fuck you*'s. I'd only ever seen them delivered to other people.

Packages slipped and jostled. "Congratulations," I told him. "Who's the lucky girl?"

"Very funny," he said.

Everything was tentative, but they were looking at some time after the summer. Los Angeles. It depended on schedules and timing. They were waiting and seeing.

I didn't say anything.

He gave me the nicest smile. "But you'll be there, right?" he asked. "I mean, whenever it is."

He was something else.

"You're something else," I told him finally.

He stopped and pointed up. I followed his gesture.

Apparently we were at the hotel he'd picked out.

Heat waves refused to roll up the back of my neck. Something like calm settled over me.

"I'll be there," I said, dumping my packages down around our feet. "I wouldn't miss it for the world." He looked a little concerned for the welfare of the packages. I thought of my mother's face, unsettled at his first marriage. Or mine, at this next one. But I'd be there. I'd smile and throw rice. I'd pose for pictures, and I'd wait.

I'd wait for him to turn around and find himself, once again, with his sister ready to jump. I'd wait because I knew that feeling that couldn't be imitated or duplicated or tricked into being. That ecstatic friction, that violence against family.

I took his face in my hands. I told him to keep his eyes open, and I kissed him. Our eyelashes were practically touching. It hurt to look at him that close up. In his eyes, I saw my reflection. And my legacy, my inheritance, what I'd made, what I deserved.

LIGHT AS A FEATHER

MACKEY CONLON DIDN'T BELIEVE IN GOD OR SCIENCE. SHE believed in patterns in the world you had to be sharp enough to catch. Feelings you had to be open enough to feel. She wasn't one of those crunchy freaks; she just believed in the ability to see things for yourself. Who else was going to watch out for you? So when, on the Sunday night four days before Christmas, a warm front invaded and hailstones began to pelt the house, she saw it as a sign. Her husband, Taylor, told her it was nothing, just hail. Did he need remind her that they lived on a big mountain in Vermont?

He was a lawyer. He talked like that. She tried not to hold it against him.

It was nine thirty. She went to the window. Some of the hailstones were the size of peas, some of jawbreakers. They bounced off the icy snow. In the winter, you could see across the back field to Sam and Patty Coe's place.

They had two sets of twins. The hail stopped midway across the field.

She tapped the glass to get Taylor's attention. "*They're* not getting hailed on," she said.

She tried not to envy the Coes their abundant family, but every time she brought them up, she could feel Taylor steeling himself, readying his arguments about their own blessings. One side of his family was Quaker. He believed in blessings and everyone getting their say. When he had something really important to talk to her about, he stood, as if in a meetinghouse.

He joined her at the window. "Huh," he said. "Weird." He said it as if he didn't think it was weird at all. His last name was Whittredge. His family's primary mode was taking things in stride. There wasn't a problem that couldn't be handled. All the men in his family sounded as if they'd been named after dogs. There were no men in her family.

The baby kicked, as if reminding her that she should talk: Mackey was a ridiculous name, a nickname from a women's rugby league in high school. Her real name was Edith. She didn't like it, either.

Most days, even since sailing through the first trimester, she felt ungenerous and small-minded. She'd said something about it to her mother once, and her mother had said, "What do you expect? Six miscarriages in four years. Fake baby-making scientific hoo-ha. How else are you supposed to feel?"

Her mother's comment had made her want to curl up in her mother's lap and hang up on her at the same

time. Her mother could always be counted on to rati-
fy the way Mackey was secretly feeling about herself,
though four years of marriage and therapy were beginning to suggest that maybe Mackey deserved to believe
in something more than, or different from, herself.

Taylor was banging around the kitchen hunting for
candles, "just in case." "Eureka," he said to himself, and she
heard the matches shake in their box and then watched
him walk back to her. Once when he'd been renovat-
ing and downstairs installing the bathroom floor, he'd
thought he was alone, but she'd been lying on their bed
listening to him work. She'd heard a terrific crash, and sat
up, ready to call out, and then he'd imitated the static of
a loudspeaker. "Houston," he said. "We have a problem."

Now on days when she looked at him unable to understand how they were going to negotiate a life together, she
brought out that moment and fell in love with him again.

"Ssh," she said.

The moon lit the driveway and yard. In the big oak,
an owl. Its head was swiveled to the left, as if making a
point of ignoring her.

The baby was arching and twisting like a toddler
having a tantrum. Her due date was eight days away.

"I know," she said softly, to her belly. "I see it."

Taylor was next to her. "Hey," he said, "an owl."

"Ssh," she said.

"He can't hear us," he said.

"Of course he can," she said.

"He's beautiful," he said.

"He's a sign of death," she said.

Taylor seemed genuinely perplexed. "Owls?" he said. "Really? Where'd you read that?"

She was crying. "Reading isn't the only way to *know* things," she said. "I just know it."

She didn't have to check to see how he was looking at her. She'd been crying a lot the last few months. He'd told her that she deserved this baby and this life. She believed that he believed that about her, and it moved her. *He* moved her. But she didn't believe it herself. And here was a hailstorm and an owl to tell her she'd been right all along. A life like this was possible, but not for her.

The next morning the hail and the owl were gone.

"See?" Taylor said. "Nothing to worry about."

She tried to let herself be calmed. She pushed her big belly gently from one side and then the other.

"The baby's not moving," she said.

Taylor was in the bathroom, running the shower. "Sleeping," he said. "Resting up for the big day."

She heard the shower curtain open and close. She watched the steam from the bathroom snake into the room. She realized with surprise that turned to fear that she'd slept through the whole night. She hadn't had an entire night's sleep in the last two months, the baby working her womb like someone making pizza.

She lay very still. Sometimes that worked. Nothing.

She called the doctor. He told her it was probably nothing, but if she was worried, if it would make her feel better, she should just come on in for an ultrasound. "We're here to make you feel better," he said.

She did not want to feel better. She'd lost six babies. She'd gone through the first trimester on tiptoe. Her lip had a raw spot from her picking at it. Even into the third trimester, she hadn't been able to celebrate. Life with her mother had taught her that when things looked good it was only because they were about to get bad.

She'd been in the exam room only three days ago. She tried to be reassured by the routine. Shirt up. Cold goop. Ultrasound slipping around on her belly.

There was her baby, perfect and curled. A girl. When you did as many procedures as they'd done, you knew more than you'd ever thought possible about someone who hadn't yet entered the world. They'd named her months ago but hadn't told anyone.

Taylor squeezed her hand.

The doctor moved the ultrasound around. And then he stopped. He held her wrist and when she looked up at him, she knew.

...

She'd met her husband at the public library in Bath, Maine. He'd been staying at his family's summer house—"the cottage," they called the place she'd always thought was a hotel—and studying for the bar. She'd been living in the town where she'd always lived, working at the library, trying to stay out of the way of an ex-boyfriend and practicing treating her body like a temple. She hadn't had a drink or drug in three months when Taylor piled a stack of books in front of her, his childhood library card in his hand.

They'd noticed each other again at the bar. Her bartending job had been her test: if she could stay sober there, she was home free.

He'd been dragged in by some friends. They had the giddy look of boys being bad. The other bartender rolled his eyes at her. She rolled hers back. The townie girl/summer boy romance was a joke. Even her mother had given up on that get-ahead plan.

One of the friends had lined up shot after shot of Cuervo Gold for him. Another had gotten her number for him. She still didn't know why she'd given it.

He called two days later at eleven in the morning, and she'd been asleep. She heard voices in the background, and then a door closing, and then nothing. And then he'd asked her out in what she'd learn was the slow, careful way he did everything. He'd never slept with anyone else in his entire life. She found that out at the reproductive clinic when they both had to fill out a fertility history. She'd repeated it to herself, sometimes out loud.

And then he'd passed the bar, and gotten the right kind of job representing people like her in Vermont, and had asked her to come with him, and she had, working on her photography, finding a job as an art teacher at a local private school.

Their story bored her. Their infertility bored her. It was the same as a million other people's, some of whom she'd met in waiting rooms, all eyeing each other, as if there were only so many babies and the criteria for getting one hadn't been made clear.

There'd been only one surprise along the way. They'd tried *on their own to no avail*—Taylor's language again. And then they'd gone to Dr. Breedlove. "Doctor *Breedlove?*" her mother had said. But to Mackey, he was just a guy from the South who'd given her friend Ginny triplets, and Sue from the store twins, and Priscilla at the bank a single on the way. She didn't care about his name. Somewhere there was a room filled with healthy babies, and he had the key.

So there'd been tests for both of them. They'd gone to the office for the results. Mackey had thought of it as the Laying-of-Blame visit. Your ovaries are shriveled, your fallopian tubes deathtraps: what made you think you deserved a baby?

She'd said, sitting there, "Her insides were a rocky place where my seed could find no purchase."

Taylor put a hand on her shoulder. He'd never seen *Raising Arizona*. She'd watched it after every miscarriage, curled up on the couch in the middle of the night, the volume down low.

He palmed the back of her head with his big hand. If he'd been born in a different class, he might've been a basketball player with seven children from six different women.

They already knew she had scar tissue from some fallopian fibroids she'd had removed. But Taylor, it turned out, had what Dr. Breedlove called "challenged swimmers." His sperm had to work hard and some of them weren't up to the job.

"Huh," Taylor had said.

There was a procedure they could try that might work.

"Might?" Mackey had asked.

Dr. Breedlove looked her way as if having to remind himself she was in the room. "Sorry. You're right. Let's stay positive here. That's half the battle. *Will* work."

And on the way home, Taylor kept saying he couldn't believe it until Mackey started to feel insulted.

"What's your thrust here?" she said. "You're shocked it was you instead of me? You couldn't imagine a problem coming from somewhere other than your recovering addict wife?"

He stared at her. "I don't know what you're talking about," he said.

She didn't either. Where did these things come from? She thought about how to apologize.

"It's not really about you," he said.

"I know," she said.

"Okay then," he said.

He held the steering wheel at ten and two, his shoulders up around his ears.

She put her head in his lap. He was wearing work boots. When he got home, he would split wood. She had a lawyer husband who stacked wood and had built his own house. How had that happened to her? Why wasn't she more grateful?

"Sorry," she said into his thigh.

He put his hand on her hip. "It's okay," he said.

He was a good person. If the procedure didn't work, he would be the strong one. He would take care of her.

They checked into the hospital they'd toured months before. They saw the same nurses, though this time there was no joking and teasing. Everyone was super-efficient, as if Mackey and Taylor were hospital inspectors there to catalog flaws.

An IV was begun, a bag of saline and another of Pitocin to start her labor. She was hooked to a monitor. Down the hall, a woman cried out.

She looked up at the nurse. "How long is this going to take?" she asked.

The nurse wrapped a warm hand around her ankle. "Can't really predict," she said. "Just like a regular delivery."

After an epidural and hours of contractions she couldn't feel, she was awake. "We've made a mistake," she said.

Taylor was sitting in a scoop chair next to her. "What, sweetie?" he asked.

"She's alive," she said.

He stood and put his palm to her forehead. "She's not," he said.

She took his hand and held it against her belly. "I *feel* her," she said.

He rested his head against hers. "Whatever you feel, it isn't her," he said.

His parents had paid for it all. Dr. Breedlove had explained chromosome paints and shown them pictures, a long probe puncturing her egg like she'd once seen a magician's needle puncture a balloon.

When she'd been a child, her mother had thrown a Halloween party where Mackey had been It for a game of Light as a Feather, Stiff as a Board. The feeling of being lifted off the ground by her mother's fingers had made her dizzy with pleasure.

Nora Louise was born on Tuesday, December 24. Six pounds, seven ounces. Twenty-one inches long. Perfect, with her father's long torso and her mother's stubby toes.

The nurse cleaned her off, swaddled her, and handed her to Mackey. "You take as long as you need," she said to both of them. She stood there for a minute, all of them looking down at Nora, still and quiet in her white flannel hospital blanket.

Years from now, she would still be there, in that bed, holding her baby girl.

The nurse wiped at her eyes. "You call me when you're ready," she said, touching both of them lightly on their arms.

Two normal embryos had been implanted: one stayed, growing and growing. There'd been celebratory calls and visits from Taylor's family. Even Mackey's mother had been happy for them, though she'd turned down an invitation to visit, saying she had too much going on. In the background, Mackey heard the latest New Friend changing channels.

"Come on," Mackey had said. "You can see me pregnant."

"Oh, Mackey," her mother said. "I've seen that before." And Mackey's hope that a baby would make everything better had started to give just a little.

"What do you think she'll be like?" Taylor had taken to asking, late at night or early in the morning, lying in bed, circling her belly button with his finger.

Mackey always shrugged, not wanting to admit that she hadn't thought about it at all. Instead she'd marveled at the changes she was undergoing. Not just shape and size, but a kind of narrowing of vision. As if pregnancy were the equivalent of giving up photography for miniature painting. She imagined the world sharing her new focus.

Now, holding her dead baby, she couldn't imagine what she'd found compelling about herself. She felt like hanging a sign, warning others away.

They dressed her in the jumper and cardigan that Taylor's sister had knitted. Purple, the color of Maine sunsets, his sister had said, but now all Mackey saw was bruise.

"Take her out of it," she said. "It's ugly."

"Okay," Taylor said. He undressed her and laid her on the bed. He searched through the duffel he'd brought and came out with an old-fashioned dress that they'd found at the Goodwill. He cradled Nora's head, pulling the dress over it. He helped one arm, then the other, into the tiny cap sleeves. The pinks of the dress reflected off her pale skin as if she'd spent the day in a brisk wind.

Both of them were crying. Mackey imagined going on and doing the things she'd always done, and she could, but only if she imagined herself sobbing the entire time.

She pulled her camera from the duffel and began shooting. Taylor cradled Nora in his arms, smoothing the dress out over her tiny feet, her still-tucked-up legs.

She wanted evidence that this girl had been here. That she'd been known.

Christmas. Taylor took time off from work. They fed the dog, watered the plants, ate what they could of the platters and pans from friends and neighbors that filled the fridge. They peed, they slept.

The phone never stopped. She let it ring. Taylor answered it. From their bed, she heard him telling the story in his low voice to people who genuinely cared but whose faces she wanted to slap. But even anger required too much energy. Life went on, an affront.

Her mother called and Mackey told her not to come. There was nothing to do.

His parents came instead. After them, his sister, then his brother, both without their children. They cleaned and cooked. Taylor went for long runs, happy, she was sure, to have someone else around to babysit her.

Should we come again? they all asked. What would be best?

It doesn't matter, she told them. And it didn't.

The doctor gave them medications. To help with sleep. To take the edge off. The bottles stayed unopened, lined up on the dresser.

She didn't go into the nursery.

More snow fell. Temperatures dropped. Taylor built large, excessive fires in the wood stove. The heat was a weight on her chest. They walked around the house in their underwear. They didn't touch each other. Three weeks passed.

The call came from her mother's neighbor: her mother had been found wandering on the frozen pond in her nightie. Five in the morning. "I don't know if you keep up with our weather," the neighbor said, "but it's mighty cold up here at five in the morning."

She had a mild case of frostbite on her toes and fingers. She was in the hospital in Portland.

Mackey wasn't sure what was being asked of her, if anything. She and her mother hadn't taken care of each other in years or maybe ever. She tried to make her thick tongue formulate appropriate questions.

"Does she want me to call her?" she asked. The first time her mother had gone into the hospital, when Mackey was eight, to have, Mackey later found out, an abortion, her mother hadn't told her why she was going, just that she had to be in the hospital for what shouldn't be longer than a day or so and not to worry. Her mother had always presented worrisome situations and then told her not to worry.

The neighbor seemed as muddled as Mackey, but for different reasons. "I think, dear, she's confused about what she wants." She gave Mackey the number at the hospital and the name of the attending, and asked if Mackey wanted her to water her mother's plants.

How had Mackey been put in charge of her mother's plants? "Where's Hank?" she asked.

The neighbor cleared her throat. "He hasn't been around in quite some time now."

Mackey pondered the news. Other lives were going on all around her. She thanked the woman and told her yes, please, water the plants, and anything else she could think of. She hung up and sat staring at the phone.

Taylor came in from outside, an armful of wood up to his neck. He slammed the door with his foot and began filling the rack next to the stove.

She watched. When he was done, he stood, brushing wood chips from the front of his shirt. He looked at her. "What?"

"I think my mom's going to have to come stay here for a while," she said.

"Okay," he said without a second thought.

They gave her the nursery. Taylor dismantled the crib and the changing table, bungee-cording the pieces together, saving the screws and brackets in ziplock bags duct-taped to the ends of the crib.

Mackey painted the moss-green walls a bright yellow that was more Piece-of-Work Mother, less Tiny New Person. She took down the curtains and mobiles and replaced little hangers with adult-sized ones. She left the large black-and-white photograph she'd taken of herself and Taylor. Her mother should feel welcome, part of something.

When they were done, they sat on the couch watching the news with the sound off.

Her mother turned out to be a different person: no longer the self-sufficient narcissist and now an anxious, fluttery, and dependent narcissist. Mackey had no idea what to make of her.

The first night didn't go well. Her mother didn't sleep, wandering the house, stumbling into unfamiliar furniture, testing locked doors, muttering. It didn't matter; Mackey wasn't sleeping either. She got out of bed and took her mother back to her mother's room, using the same route each time, hoping to imprint some kind of inner map-making ability. Penelope, the dog, stopped getting up.

"I can't stay here," her mother kept saying. "Take me back."

"Sure you can," Mackey would answer, leading her down the hall.

At five in the morning, Mackey found her tapping lightly on the inside of the kitchen door. The pockets of her robe were stuffed with sugar packets. Mackey wrapped her in a wool throw. Her mother shrugged it off.

"I've got to get out of here," she said.

Mackey stood with her, looking out the half window in the door. The snow was a sickly blue. The wind that had been going all night was gone. Nothing moved.

"Where do you want to go?" she asked.

"Where do you think?" her mother said. She looked out past the snowy field to the woods, and past that to the sky. Mackey imagined them opening the door and making their escape, running across the hard snow like girls.

She tried the wool throw on her mother's shoulders again. A lifetime of drinking and smoking had turned her mother's body into something sharp and hard. Mackey rubbed the thin shoulders. "This is home," she said.

Her mother asked if she remembered the time she didn't want to take a bath.

Mackey knew the reference. She'd been ten. She didn't remember why she hadn't wanted to bathe. They'd been visiting someone with a beach house her mother was trying to date. Her mother had dragged her down the hallway by both arms. Mackey had knocked paintings and pictures off the walls.

Now her mother patted her robe pockets for cigarettes. "Whose house was that?" she asked. "That was a nice place."

Mackey led her to the table and pulled a chair out. She opened a bottom drawer and dug around, coming up with a pack of cigarettes she'd hidden years ago. She lit one for her mother, and one for herself.

"Frank Moody," she said.

"I think you're right," her mother said, exhaling. "Frank Moody," she repeated, watching the smoke curl up out of her mouth.

...

And for the next two weeks sometimes her mother was there and sometimes she wasn't. Sometimes, they woke to the smell of eggs and bacon and fresh biscuits, the table set. Sometimes, they woke to the door wide open, her mother in the car, trying to start it with the house key.

Most days were days of ordinary flatness. They did jigsaw puzzles and crosswords, her mother pretending to help with both. Taylor shoveled the walk, the two women scattering salt behind him. Her mother leafed through the newspaper. Mackey clipped her mother's finger and toenails and rubbed lotion into her hands and feet. She filled the humidifiers. Her mother watered the plants and talked to the dog. She cooked meals Mackey had no idea she knew how to make. She cleaned the venetian blinds in the bathroom one slat at a time. At the grocery she got in an argument with the man at the deli counter and said afterward that she knew what kind of person he was.

And driving home, Mackey understood that the flatness wasn't ordinary; it was a heavy weight, a cast-iron lid, trying to hold everything down.

At one point they saw her mother halfway across the field digging small holes in the snow with the heel of her slipper. Taylor pulled his boots on and trudged out to get her.

Two weeks later, he took Mackey aside in the kitchen. "We can't live like this forever," he said.

All through elementary school, when the bus got to her stop, someone would say, "You *live* here?"

"Like what?" Mackey asked.

He glanced around as if the answer were in the kitchen. "She can't be happy," he said. He paused as if he'd forgotten what he was talking about. "We need help," he finally added.

"Then *do* something," she said.

The night before the autopsy results were due back, her mother wanted to give her a makeover.

Taylor had gone to bed hours before, since any kind of anxiety made him sleepy. Mackey knew she'd be up for hours. "I don't think so," she told her mom.

Her mother had her red fake leather case open on the kitchen table, its trays expanded like bleachers. It looked like a model of a football stadium. "Tools of the trade," she'd said when Mackey poked through it as a girl.

"Come on," her mother said. "I'll do your face. We'll paint each other's nails. You can watch bad TV."

"Bad TV is bad for you," Mackey said.

Her mother was lining up bottles of polish. She gave one a hard shake and frowned at her daughter. "How did I get a daughter like you?" she asked. "Sometimes I wonder."

"That makes two of us," Mackey said.

"I'm sure it does," her mother said. She regarded her daughter. "To be honest," she said, "your face could use some doing."

"Mom," Mackey said. "If we were going to list each other's problems…"

Her mother held a hand up. "Don't get mad. I'm just being a friend, telling the truth." She dug around in her box. "Nothing I can't fix," she said.

Her mother liked to sum up her maternal philosophy every so often by saying, "I'm your friend, not your mother." She didn't believe in behavior based on genetic responsibility; she believed in free will. She said whatever she did, she did because she wanted to and Mackey shouldn't expect anything else.

For a long time, Mackey had thought it was a liberated way to think.

This time it seemed important not to let it pass. This time Mackey said, "I don't need a friend. I don't want to be friends with you."

"Don't be ridiculous," her mother said. "Of course you do."

The next day they got the results: a compromised connection between umbilical cord and placenta, a freak occurrence, nothing to do with their previous miscarriages, nothing to indicate that the next baby would be anything but healthy.

"I wish I'd had a reason to do a C-section," Dr. Breedlove said. "She would've been fine."

Mackey by that point had been a balloon inflated and deflated too many times. She didn't even note the cruelty of his comment. That would be for friends to point out later. She thought of a frayed end of her umbilical cord, all that life leaking out around it, surrounding Nora, unreachable. Had she starved to death? Had all that movement she'd felt the night before been her daughter in agony?

Back home, her mother had emptied the contents of the fridge and the freezer and stacked everything against the wall in her room. She was sleeping on her back in her bed, her mouth open, snoring softly. Since she'd been there, she hadn't mentioned Nora once.

Taylor returned all the food to its proper place and went for a run. He was training for a marathon. Taylor, silly Taylor.

Mackey went to the kitchen table and stared at the sandwich he'd left her. Penelope lumbered in. Mackey held the sandwich out on the flat of her hand as if she were feeding a horse.

The owl was back. In the middle of the day. The sun on the snow was painful. He was on the same branch as before, but this time looking straight at her. He stayed like that for forty-five minutes, never taking his big yellow eyes off her. Then he spread his wings and headed right for her, veering up and over the roof at the last minute.

She didn't want reasonable explanations. It was the middle of a sunny day. The same owl. He'd stared at her for forty-five minutes. She turned these facts over and over. She didn't know what to believe; then she did. That owl had been Nora, there to give her something. She just didn't know what.

. . .

When her mother woke up, Mackey led her downstairs to the darkroom. "Keep me company," she said. Taylor had surprised her by converting the back room for their first anniversary.

She settled her mother in a chair and took out the roll of film of Nora.

"It's very dirty," her mother said. Her face these last weeks had softened. It was like dough dusted with flour.

Mackey shrugged and kept at her work. She hadn't been in there in months, afraid of what the chemicals could do to the baby.

Her mother looked around, anxious. "Where are we?"

"We're here, in the darkroom, in the house, in Burlington, Vermont, in the United States of America," Mackey said.

Her mother wasn't reassured. Mackey supposed she was right not to be. Upstairs, Taylor's footsteps, the paired thumps of his sneakers being tossed into the corner.

"We're just here," Mackey said. "Here is safe. Come on."

Her mother joined her at the table, the three white enamel trays in a row in front of them.

The first image began to appear. The pattern of the dress, the curled fingers.

Her mother held her hand to her mouth. "Oh!" she said. "What a thing. How did you do that?" she asked.

"It's just chemicals," Mackey said, pushing the floating paper here and there with the tongs, but her heart was in orbit.

The image of Nora darkened and cleared, and the two women bent over her.

"It's magic," her mother said.

Mackey was crying. Her mother wiped the tears with her sleeve and said, "Poor, poor baby." Nora regarded them from behind closed lids.

Her mother tapped the table with her fingertips and looked around as if seeing the place for the first time, her voice echoing the rhythm of her hands. "Here we are. Here we are. Here we are."

DON'T KNOW WHERE,
DON'T KNOW WHEN

PEOPLE WHO DIDN'T KNOW BETTER ENVIED ZIZI. SHE HAD A cool nickname, an exotic Asian mixed-race pedigree, and some guy who seemed to pay the bills in a pinch. She dressed East Village extreme (shredded leggings, careless boots, layers and layers); her bangs were Mamie Eisenhower, her complexion was Louise Brooks, her jewelry was vintage. She was twentysomething. Her body was Japanese teen, but dark chocolate and single-malt scotch were an everyday thing. It was unclear how she made a living. She had circles under her eyes, but the dabbling in heroin was years ago. Early childhood development. She was an only child, and knew everyone, but not even her guy had seen her cry. Her father lived in a faraway country and was vaguely famous, but no one could remember for what. Her mother was kind and easy to deceive. Her apartment was throwback tenement with exposed brick walls and a bathtub in the kitchen. Her guy bought it for her. It was directly below the one he shared with his wife. For convenience, he said at the time. Why be getting *to* when I could just be getting, he said, smiling at his own bad joke and spreading her legs, the sounds of his wife walking above them, doing the ironing, or the dishes, or whatever it was that wives did, making Zizi flush with heat.

Now, four years after that and a month after his death, the sounds of his wife, her name is Mabel, make Zizi freeze and flatten like a cat alert to danger, even though other than the day the towers went down (the guy he was having breakfast with was the last man on the last elevator that made it down, and Zizi has spent way too much time imagining how that all shook out), Mabel has shown only occasional interest in her. This is fine with her, since she's not the kind of person it's useful to rely on. She'll say yes and then end up meaning no. The level of her self-consciousness about this was for a while a topic of discussion among her acquaintances. Maybe it was an Asian thing. Now it's just something they keep in mind as they make their plans, the way they do with their vegan friends or the ones who can't drive.

She simultaneously believes herself to be in no way enviable and the most interesting person in the room. Very early in their relationship, surprising herself, she told Oliver that she was a constant bundle of need. He laughed, resting his hand on her thigh in his joy. But the few people over the years who have paid attention have known not to laugh. A high school teacher took her aside after she'd gone to a school Halloween party as a prostitute and told her that other kids listened to her and what she told the world about herself was what the world was going to believe. Her mother after a particularly horrible high school party had stroked her cheek and said, no questions, no recriminations, "Burn the dress."

Zizi would've said that no one else knew what kind of guy her married man was. She would've said that there was no one but herself to remind her that in the long run, perhaps what had happened was best, and no one but herself to believe it. But now there was Mabel. Mabel complicated everything.

After the first tower fell, Zizi rushed to open her apartment door without knowing why. Maybe he hadn't been at that breakfast meeting; maybe he'd been waiting in the hall. Instead Mabel was standing there. Zizi had only ever seen her in passing, glimpses of straight blonde hair beneath a creamy knit hat. Sometimes Zizi leaned out her window to watch the two of them walk down the street, the tops of their heads a tiny uncharted archipelago below. In the hallway, Mabel seemed more beautiful than usual, and looked at her, focusing. "Who are you?" she asked.

Once, Zizi had asked him what she was supposed to do if she ran into Mabel in the building. "Nothing," Oliver had said. "You're the woman downstairs."

"You're on my landing," she finally said now.

Mabel looked around her feet in a small sweep. "So?" she said.

She wasn't wearing shoes. Her mouth was small and round. Her eyes were huge. "You have huge eyes," Zizi said.

"I know," Mabel said, and started weeping. Oliver had told Zizi that his wife never cried from sadness, only from anger and frustration. "My husband was in that building," Mabel said.

He'd been inside Zizi less than two hours before and had told Mabel his meeting started earlier than it did. "And she believes you?" Zizi had said, taking his finger, wrapping it with hers, putting both inside her.

"What's not to believe?" he said, slipping his hand away, flipping her onto her belly, hinging her at the hips to meet him.

"Stay," she said when he'd finished, and he'd smiled and kissed her, his mouth tasting of the both of them, but he'd climbed over her, reaching for his clothes. "'Should I stay or should I go?'" he said. He liked talking in song lyrics. He was in advertising and liked to break the world into smaller and smaller shards. He swore he could design an ad for nothing with no dialogue, no images, and no sound. On good days, she thought of her life as some kind of avant-garde opera, and on bad ones, she thought of it the same way.

When he pulled his T-shirt over his head the workings of his muscles beneath his pale skin always took her by surprise, as if someone had startled her trying to cure her of hiccups.

"'I don't know why you say goodbye, I say hello,'" she said.

He came back to the bed and put his hand between her legs. He liked it when she played his games. "Listen," he said. "I've got someone else I want you to meet."

He slipped his fingers inside her and moved them slowly. She tried to stay still and silent. "I think you'll like him," he said, nudging her breast with his nose. His voice was liquid and warm. She imagined it covering her like slow-flow lava.

"I want everyone to know how gorgeous you are," he said. "'All the best cowboys have Chinese eyes,'" he said, climbing on top of her, putting himself inside of her, giving her what she wanted for now.

The sounds of the television filtered onto the landing. She looked at Mabel and suggested they could watch the news together. They could be here for when he came home.

Mabel regarded her like maybe she was retarded. "Did you see that building fall?" she said. "He was at the top of it."

Then her expression changed. "Did you know him?"

Zizi shook her head, something in her throat.

"He's an asshole," Mabel said flatly.

He had once said he admired his wife's bluntness. He said she had asked his best friend about a new girlfriend and how the initial intercourse had gone. He had laughed, remembering, his fingers playing with Zizi's hair.

"I ask stuff like that," Zizi said.

He laughed again, but differently, and said the jury was still out. She had gone to get another cup of coffee, something to get her body back up to speed.

...

The women stood there. And then Zizi said, "Well, do you want to come in anyway?" And Mabel did, and they sat on the couch and watched the news. They watched the falling men and women, and both of them tried silently to pick him out.

At some point, it was night, and one of them muted the sound and returned to the couch. Mabel's phone rang several times above them. Two people climbed the stairs and rang her doorbell.

They sat in the dark, their skin lit by the television, and Zizi remembered bedtimes endlessly postponed when her mother, lost in the late show, forgot about her curled at the other end of the couch.

Mabel finally said again that he was an asshole, and it was as if after all their waiting, he had finally walked through the door, shaking his head and saying what a day he had had.

The bedroom was a crime scene, but Zizi realized they hadn't spent much time in the other parts of the apartment. "The good kind of asshole or the asshole kind?" she asked.

Mabel looked at her again the way she had in the hallway. Zizi pulled her knees up. "Some girls can make the whole asshole thing work for them," she said, her voice sounding not quite her own.

"Some girls are idiots," Mabel said sadly. "Or worse."

Zizi wanted to know what she meant, and now she wishes she'd asked, but that had been a month ago, and since then, there's been a kind of embarrassment on both their parts, as if they'd walked in on each other in the bathroom.

. . .

For the past few days, she's been hearing footsteps upstairs in Mabel's apartment. She thinks she can make out a male voice. Sometimes she lies in her bed listening, wondering what she wishes for the woman.

After he died she got a temp job, enough to pay the bills. She sees friends and is festive enough to keep them from worrying. But the sight of his toothbrush, the spray of worn bristles like a tiny flayed thing, can still take her breath. She's found herself walking the city sure she can smell him. And then she spends more time surprised and disoriented that this was how she spent her day. *Really?* she thinks. *Really?*

But she feels the possibility of reinvention in her bloodstream like a drug. She looks at other men now, the ones with kind eyes who always seemed to occupy another time zone, and thinks, *Why not?*

A week ago she went to the funeral his parents had finally agreed to have and sat in the last pew, studying the backs of heads of people she'd always wanted to meet because he seemed his happiest when talking about them: his parents from Maine, his sister and her four kids, the best friend from grade school. Her gaze took in every woman within a certain age range. He had been forty-three. She was twenty-six, and she figured his parameters had been wider than that.

She listened to the eulogies and heard new information without learning anything useful. He had mastered a two-wheeler when he was three; he'd hidden under an armchair one Christmas Eve; his parents hadn't wanted him to move to New York; he loved orange soda. There was one guy from Africa, some kind of exchange student he had sponsored, whose eulogy was all about generosity. She listened like a dog trying to hear registers just out of range.

For reasons she still doesn't understand she went through the receiving line, taking his parents' hands in hers. His mother acknowledged her in unfocused ways.

At the end of the line, Mabel seemed so unsurprised to see her there that Zizi found herself hugging her. Mabel whispered, "There's no body in there. His mom told me to just get his favorite outfit."

Zizi imagined the blue plaid cowboy shirt and dark jeans flat against white satin. A boy's special occasion outfit laid out by his mother.

"Can you believe this shit?" Mabel was saying, but the line pressed Zizi forward before she had to answer.

Outside in a tree there were actual birds engaged in actual chirping. Everyone got into cars with their headlights on and she sat on the church steps and closed her eyes and tilted her face to the thin October sun. The traffic noise quieted. The breeze hit her cheeks. He had loved Vera Lynn's "We'll Meet Again." Once they'd spent the whole day in bed, him hitting *play* over and over. She thought of his low voice, and those deflated clothes in the coffin.

"You must be Zizi," a low voice said.

She opened her eyes. He was standing against the sun and she couldn't make out his features. But then he stepped aside and of course it wasn't him; it was just a guy, and she laughed once, a short, angry sound.

"I guess I must," she said, flirting despite herself.

He was a friend of Oliver's. Oliver had been planning to introduce them. The guy's black suit pants were tapered over boots with Cuban heels. His shirt was a deep green. His physiognomy was all sharp angles, and he seemed not to want to face her head on.

"The someone else," she said.

"Sorry?" he said, but she shook her head.

"Ray," he said. He reached a hand out and she took it. It was cool and dry and something like desire flexed inside of her. He held on to her longer than he should've, and she let him. He told her Oliver had been right about her.

Despite, or maybe because of, their embarrassment, she and Mabel haven't avoided each other completely. Earlier tonight, Mabel slipped a sheet of paper under her door with a Post-it attached: *Read this, would you?*

Incoherent? Totally. Mildly. Next to the choices, she had drawn two small boxes. *Check one.*

It seemed to be a perky anecdote about how Oliver had gotten several of his college friends to go midnight hiking. She called Mabel at the number she had looked up years ago. She'd told Oliver she'd done so. "What if it's an emergency," she'd argued. "Your emergencies are not my emergencies," he'd answered, but she'd quit arguing, since holding the grenade could be as powerful as throwing it.

She heard the phone upstairs and thumping across what she imagined was the living room. She said hello.

"Who is this?" Mabel said.

"Me, from downstairs," Zizi said.

"Did you read it?" Mabel asked.

"Yes," Zizi said.

"Well?" It sounded as if she were playing dominoes. A cat meowed. Zizi hadn't known they had a cat.

"I'm not really sure what you want from me on this," she said.

"It's for that thing the *Times* is doing," Mabel said. "I need someone who didn't know him at all."

Zizi offered to come up so they could go over it together.

There was a pause, and Mabel said yes, and by the time Zizi arrived, two beers had been opened and Fritos had been dumped into a bowl. The floor plan looked the same as hers, but glancing down the hall she could tell the apartment went on and on. How many apartments had he bought in this building, anyway? He could've owned the whole thing for all she knew.

In a corner, boxes were stacked against the walls. His stuff, she assumed.

She searched idly for anything of his that hadn't yet been packed up as she tried to follow Mabel's conversation.

Apparently a *Times* reporter had called to interview her for its Portraits of Grief series. Apparently Mabel had asked whether there was a Portraits of Ambivalence series.

Mabel said, "Doesn't it seem unlikely that every one of them were saints? And what's the thrust here, that we can't mourn the flawed?"

It wasn't the conversation Zizi had imagined. She hadn't really imagined the conversation at all. She had just wanted to get into this apartment, and now here she was.

"I mean, how many saints do you know?" Mabel asked.

Zizi was Asian enough to answer questions when they were asked of her. She said, "Not that many, I guess."

"Good girl," Mabel said.

Good girl, Oliver had told her the first time she agreed to meet one of his friends. He'd whispered that in her ear, kneeling by the bed while the other guy made his way around her like a blind man moving down an unfamiliar hallway.

Mabel was looking at her. Clearly, something was expected of her.

"I would imagine that people are feeling all sorts of things about the people they lost," Zizi said.

Mabel looked over her shoulder as if rolling her eyes about Zizi with someone else. He had liked to do the same thing.

What did she think? She'd been his soul mate, his one true love? She'd always recognized what she was doing as a kind of degradation, but it had been *her* degradation, a certain kind of power. What had she thought: An Emperor of the Universe would have stopped having affairs once he met her? And none of this was news, so what *else* was going on with her?

"So why didn't you leave him?" Zizi asked, sounding angrier than she'd meant to.

Mabel looked sad. "Nice tone," she said quietly.

Zizi said, "Well? Why didn't you?"

Mabel's face was suddenly that of a four-year-old's. She was quiet. Finally, she said, "Leaving is hard."

Zizi did not want to feel sorry for anyone. She said, "You haven't even said what made him so terrible. You just keep saying asshole asshole asshole."

The cat jumped up into Mabel's lap. They both faced Zizi. "How's Ray?" Mabel asked.

Zizi blushed, which she almost never did. Maybe Oliver's death was going to mean nothing but surprise from here on out. She hadn't seen Ray since the funeral, but they'd talked on the phone. "He's fine," she said. She wondered if Ray had told Mabel. She realized she might never know what Mabel knew and how she knew it.

She stood and gestured at the paper on the table. "I think you're all set with that. I'd better go," she said.

"Have you slept with him yet?" Mabel asked.

Zizi was happy not to have to lie and shook her head. "This is a strange conversation," she said.

"This is what all my conversations are like," Mabel said.

It made sense. What kind of woman would the Emperor of the Universe marry?

"Ray's not really in your wheelhouse," Mabel said, not unkindly.

"You don't know anything about me," Zizi said. Even as she said it, she understood it might not be true.

Mabel started to say something and then crossed her arms like a flower closing for the night. "You're right," she said. "But he's a different beast altogether."

Zizi registered the care in her voice, and thanked her, and let herself out, and spent hours thinking about who was in whose wheelhouse. She heard the cat all night and marveled that she'd never heard it before.

He had introduced her to three friends before Ray. Always in hotels, always in the lost hours between late night and early morning. She had vetoed her apartment, drawing the line somewhere to prove that she could. She also told him she wanted his guarantee she wouldn't run into any of these guys. He had agreed to everything as if he could actually supply it.

She thought of the encounters as adventures under-taken by the fierce and brave. She had been a cautious child. High swings had made her nervous. She would walk along the low stone walls of her neighborhood, but would drop to her knees to climb down. She hadn't liked team sports and had been a Good Asian as a student, adept at assignments and winning the approval of her teachers. She had been competent at long-distance swimming, and had liked the weightlessness of it, the isolation, the gratifying rewards of stamina and subterranean stores of energy. She had loved the way her body became unrecognizable, her skin wrinkled like something animal and new.

He hadn't wanted her to just lie there. He wanted her to enjoy it. And so she'd thought of fucking his friends while he watched as being like swimming across a wide lake. She closed her eyes and moved beneath the surface in ways that suggested pleasure and power. Occasionally she opened her eyes and turned her head to find him. And there he always was. You're gorgeous, he would say. He would tell her what the two of them would do later, on their own, for the rest of their lives, the other guy's sweat falling on her from above. What did I tell you? he'd say to his friend, taking his shoulder. Was I right, or was I right?

She calls Ray at four in the morning. She tells him she wants to see him. Enough of these phone calls, she says.

She can hear him wherever he lives, whatever kind of sheets and blankets he's got on whatever kind of bed, trying to pull himself to clarity. He clears his throat and she says, "If you don't know who this is, the offer's withdrawn."

His voice is wonderfully logged with sleep. "Oh, I know who you are," he says.

"Guys," she says with disgust. "They always know everything."

She throws her own covers off and stretches her legs, pointing and flexing her feet. She tells him she's naked. She's not.

"Me, too," he says.

"Liar," she says. "You sleep in a T-shirt that your college ultimate Frisbee team won off your archrivals. You still remember the day. When you come over, you're going to bring it with you. You don't like to sleep naked. You don't much like sleeping except when you're alone, but in the morning, you're going to tell me that you've never fallen asleep faster. And that trust is an issue for you."

"Uncanny," he says blandly.

He muffles the phone and she hears him talking.

"Hello?" she says.

"Hello," he says.

"Are you with someone?" she asks.

His voice is muffled again. She makes out "that girl."

He's back. "Hey," he says, all muscle and charm.

She's not sure if this changes things or not, but it seems even more important to find out.

"Taking guys away from other women is my specialty," she says.

The other woman is still talking. He's silent, and she's not sure how long she should wait. She pulls the covers up, and says, "What are you *doing*?" She lies there, a stupid, graceless thing, and then she hangs up.

The summer she was twelve she volunteered at a day camp for preschoolers. One little girl had driven all the counselors crazy with her neediness and whining. No one but Zizi could comfort her, and not even she could do it consistently. Some days, her tricks worked, others they didn't. But when they worked, she felt as if something real had been accomplished, and both girls went home feeling better about themselves.

By the end of the summer, the girl had grown up a little and gotten better at handling her own needs. Zizi doesn't remember the circumstances, but she does remember the corner of the playground where she slapped the girl's hand in order for there to be tears, in order for there to be the need for comfort. She remembers the girl after some hesitation allowing herself to receive the care offered from the person who had created its need. Over the years, the moment has come back to her often enough to indicate something, but Zizi doesn't know what.

When he shows up at her door, she doesn't know whether to feel triumphant or pathetic. She decides on triumphant and lets him in.

"Where's your friend?" she asks.

He's wearing pressed jeans and a fitted white T-shirt. He doesn't look anything like thrown together. "Like you," he says. "Sad, angry, and all alone."

A small motor whirs to life in her chest while he smiles and tilts his head at her. "*I'm* not alone," she says.

They stand there. Outside dawn is creeping over the buildings. The apartment is the blue of deep water. Upstairs Mabel is walking around. She's up at this hour every day. The guy looks at Zizi. She can't read his expression.

"Uh-uh," he says. "No changing your mind now."

She feels as if she's the apartment with more rooms than she knew she had. Doors close inside of her.

"What am I thinking now?" she asks. She really wants to know.

He moves toward her without answering. Here she was believing she was taking a curtain call, and it turns out the house lights are up, the audience gone.

"Listen," she begins, but one of his hands gently covers her mouth and his other circles her arm.

"If I scream, Mabel will hear me," she says through his fingers.

He takes his hand away and waves his fingers. "You're not going to scream," he says. "Even you know that."

She has no idea what's next. "I want you to leave," she says.

He drops his hand and stares. "No, you don't," he says, as if speaking to a child he's decided to treat like an adult.

"Poor little Geisha Girl," he says, lifting her nightshirt up and over her head. "Doesn't even know what she wants." He gentles her down to the floor, and then stands to undress. She could get up. She lies there, watching him.

Naked, he lowers himself on top of her, spreading her legs with his knees. He presses his weight along her and stops his face so close to hers that her vision blurs. "Do you *want* to know?" he asks.

He shifts his hips and he's inside her.

She hooks one leg over his back and twists, trying to turn them over. He won't let her. He smiles as if he can't be surprised, pulls her arms up over her head, puts her wrists in one of his hands, and quiets her.

She's crying. She can't believe she's crying in front of this asshole. But she wants to hear what he's got to say, and that makes her cry harder.

He licks her tears from the corners of her eyes. His mouth settles against her ear.

He pushes into her, and her skin chafes against the floor. He's stopped talking. As soon as she wraps her other leg around him he rolls off, lying on his back beside her. They both lie there looking up at the ceiling.

"Mabel's awake," he says.

Zizi imagines her peering through a hole in her floor, taking in the scene. *Some girls are idiots*, Zizi thinks.

"She seems to be doing pretty well," he says. He brushes a finger down her belly and between her legs. She shivers at its offhanded intimacy. "Don't you think?" he asks.

"I wouldn't know," she says.

"Exactly," he says. "Poor Zizi. Spends her life as the tower, when all she's ever wanted was to be the plane."

"Nice simile," she manages. "Weren't you his friend?"

"Weren't you?" he says. He seems to lose interest in the question.

Years ago, a professor guessed what high school she had gone to, and she had refused to believe that he hadn't checked her file, that he didn't have inside information. He had laughed and told her that maybe she wasn't the enigma she imagined. The possibility had thrilled and shaken her.

Ray's nonchalance is like a wave receding to reveal the hard, wet sand. The effortlessness of his understanding and its indifference break her heart.

She gets on top of him.

"Back for more?" he asks.

She presses her chest to his. From above, Mabel would see a weighty, solid thing.

He teases at her mouth with his own. He wets his finger and runs it down the center of her rear. He puts his finger in her ass.

She tucks her legs up alongside him like a marsupial and apologizes to herself. She doesn't know any better. She knows this to be both the truth and its opposite.

"At least I know that," she says out loud.

"What?" he asks.

She doesn't answer. She takes that same finger, pushes it into his mouth and holds it there. A small sound escapes him, maybe one of surprise, and they begin the song and dance, and she thinks that if Mabel ever asks, she'd be able to tell her that we can mourn the flawed; we can, and we do.

GIRLS ONLY

ONE SUMMER WHEN THEY WERE ALL STILL FRIENDS, THEY were the bridesmaids, determined for once to do their best. Their jobs were to smile and fuss, offer agreement and an extra set of hands. They were to play at intimacy, past and present. They were to overlook that they hadn't been close in any way for the past five years. While they believed the bride belonged in their little human pyramid, they also agreed she'd been bottom row. They'd seen the movies and read their Jane Austen. But they understood that this one time they were to be her backup singers, her session drummers. Her beaver posse, Cleo said on the day they arrived at the bride's childhood home for their week of pre-wedding Girl Fun, but Cleo had always said things like that. She was spacey and tone-deaf, and since college—could it already be nine years?—she had made her living as an escort. Anna, being an environmental lawyer and a former president's great-great-granddaughter, told her her remark was repulsive.

Cleo said she had been kidding. "Can't we just be nice to each other?" she added.

Gwen, the Asian, the smart one with a tendency toward the self-righteous and the cruel—the one who claimed she'd orchestrated Martha Stewart's return to greatness after her time in the hole—answered while looking at Cleo's tight minidress—and she really did have an extraordinary body, which many thought made up for her plain face—"Sure. Could you teach us how to have sex for money?"

And she didn't stop there, since it was difficult for her to keep anything of which she disapproved to herself. "Is that dress crushed velvet *and* spandex?" she asked.

The rest of them refrained from piling on. But Cleo had never been intimidated by Asians or smart people, so she said, "Some of us can wear it, and some of us can't," and gestured at Gwen's waistline and made little pinching movements with her finger and thumb.

Gwen responded that she gathered that what Cleo tended to ingest was pretty low on calories.

They'd met freshman year of college, the five of them thrown together by default when it turned out they were the only people in their dorm not auditioning for an acappella group. Some of them could sing, and they loved getting onstage as a group on karaoke night and belting out songs, but really: Acappella? And besides the lameness, who could stand all that constant harmonizing?

They'd always walked the line between teasing and cruelty. It gave their relationships energy and power, as if they'd been told to hold hands and make their way over a cable across a canyon. Holding on was hard, but letting go worse.

They were supposed to be getting ready for dinner. The house was a restored barn and farmhouse with various outbuildings that all used to be something other than what they were now. The bride's wing was the former hayloft with a fairy tale bedroom at one end and a vast living space, now transformed into guest housing for the girls, on the other. They were draped across various sofas and rugs and curled into oversized chairs like a painting of the last days of Rome. From the window seat, where she was pretending to blow her cigarette smoke out the open window, Ticien (her parents had named her after the painter, and misspelled the name) sighed. "God," she said. "You people are so—" She trailed off, losing interest.

No one had tried very hard to pin her down. She seemed to make a living doing performance art and drugs. They all did drugs, but she made a living at it.

"There's Daphne," she said, gesturing out the window.

They gathered around the window seat like children at the deep end of the pool. They still couldn't believe Daphne was the first of their group to get married. She'd been the fuckup with the screwed-up childhood (well, the more screwed-up childhood), the one they'd ushered into clothes and gotten to class, the one who'd slept with half the lacrosse team in a week their freshman year. Every night, a different guy making his way to the suite's bathroom. They thought of her as Cleo without the paycheck, and told new friends stories filled with exaggeration about how college had been all about preventing her from running into traffic. Since then, they'd kept up with her by using air quotes when asking each other who she was dating. They were never more in harmony than when talking about her, since she was the one who made them feel better about themselves.

And now there she was walking arm in arm with Jack Briggs, sixty-two, DDB advertising, born and raised in Portland, Maine, with two children older than her. When she'd told her mother his age, her mother had said, "Oh, sweetie, but what will you talk about?" Her father had sent her an ad Jack had created for Metamucil.

The bridesmaids had been surprised, since Jack was a more complicated choice than usual for her. Yes, he was thirty years older, and Ticien and Anna had agreed when they'd first met him that he had something of the Icky Guy about him. But he was also stable and calm and seemed focused on her in the best kind of way.

They'd always been circumspect when it came to her latest enthusiasms. Freshman year, they'd called her Bad Idea Teen after their favorite *Saturday Night Live* parody ad. "Well, he's an ex-freebase addict, and he's trying to turn his life around, and he needs a place to stay for a couple of months. *Bad Idea Jeans*." "Normally I wear protection, but then I thought, 'When am I gonna make it back to Haiti?' *Bad Idea Jeans*." But in the case of the Jack news, they'd told her how happy her happiness made them, and that had been the truth if not the whole truth. She was getting married, after all. They counted themselves as independent women, but even so.

So there she was, the bride, walking across her parents' Connecticut back forty as if she knew she was being watched. And there they were, watching.

"They look happy," Anna said quietly.

No one said anything else until Gwen asked if Jack had been married once or twice before. Cleo said she'd heard from Daphne's father that it was five. Anna said, "*Five?*"

Cleo said that she'd asked about it and Daphne said she wasn't worried. Daphne's logic had been, what were the chances that he'd fail at it a sixth time? She'd added that those other wives had all had their own opinions, and that she was happy to let his opinions rule the day. She was tired of her own opinions. What good had *they* ever done? She *wanted* to ride shotgun for the rest of her life.

The girls were quieted by Cleo's report, thinking it was true Daphne was less opinionated, but also true that she'd already been riding shotgun most of her life. They all knew what could happen if you got in the wrong car.

They watched some more, all of them thinking some very unbridesmaidy things, some of them ashamed of themselves and some of them not.

"Well, really," Anna finally said. "What do we know about happy?"

When Cleo hooked up with the groom on Friday, they were unsurprised, and in small, strange ways, envious. By that point in the week, they'd given up on being good, as if the bridal shower and the bachelorette Circus Camp day had been all they could manage. So on Wednesday Anna had refused the massage during Spa Day because she didn't like to get undressed and didn't like strangers touching her. On Thursday Cleo had said she'd let the dog out before bed but hadn't, and in the morning Daphne's mother spent twenty minutes cleaning the living room rug. Then Gwen and Anna had taken a long hike and were an hour late to the rehearsal dinner, wandering in sweaty and unshowered. During the drinking afterward Cleo had slid her card into the pockets of random men. And Ticien had been gone for hours after dinner only to return to the house glassy-eyed and purring.

Daphne had forgiven them all their transgressions, as she always had.

And it turned out that her claims that she hadn't done drugs since meeting Jack were looking like the truth. No one had seen her drink anything stronger than white wine all week, and she only watched as they spent the night before her wedding downing tequila shots. So by the time they stumbled their way back to their shared loft, took what they hoped would be beauty-saving doses of aspirin, drank their weight in glasses of cold water, and lay down beneath six-hundred-thread-count all-cotton sheets, they were swollen with sadness. They lay there listening to each other's breathing, feeling laden with it, asking themselves how they would bear the weekend, or the following month, or the one after that. And the more honest of them knew that time wasn't the problem.

And so they were awake when Cleo came lightly up the stairs, her sandals in her hand, her gorgeous body a silhouette in the doorway as she waited for her eyes to adjust to the dark.

"Where've you been?" Ticien asked as if she already knew, and maybe she did. She was more like Cleo than any of the others.

And at the sound of voices the rest of them gathered. Thank God, they thought. Something awake in all this quiet.

Cleo reclined on the rug, stretching her arms over her head, pointing her toes. She'd started as a stripper and had been threatening all week to do a pole dance instead of a toast. "Out," she said.

"In New Canaan, Connecticut?" Anna asked.

They sat cross-legged around her as if at a séance run by teenagers. "How old are we, anyway?" Gwen asked. She turned on a table lamp, then turned it off. The property's security lamps gave the room an orange glow.

"Just tell me it wasn't Jack," she said.

Cleo opened her eyes. "It wasn't Jack," she said, smiling.

"Oh," Anna said. She'd spent her life with them feeling like the one Catholic schoolgirl at the party.

Gwen, on the other hand, with her Chinese girl arrogance, tended to find the rest of them pathetic. "Perfect," she said.

Cleo was still smiling. She laughed and rolled her head on the carpet side to side.

Ticien said, "Why're we laughing?"

Gwen said, "We're not."

"I hear laughing," Ticien said.

Gwen turned back to Cleo. "What happened?"

"I don't know," she said. "We were in the playground." She lifted her head to look down at her belly. "I've got wood chips on me."

Years ago Daphne's father had put in a playground for her. Passersby often mistook the property for a prep school.

"The playground," Anna repeated. "What was he doing there?"

"Playing?" Cleo suggested.

Sometimes Anna hated Cleo, she really did.

While they watched, Cleo rolled onto her belly and kicked her legs lazily against her butt. "He has a huge dick," she said.

No one spoke. They might've had sex; they might've just kissed; there might've been other things involved. They might've done nothing. The girls weren't going to give her the satisfaction of trying to puzzle it out.

Outside the sky was lightening. "Daphne's wedding day," Ticien said.

Cleo shrugged. "I told him I was a professional so it barely counts as cheating, or whatever."

"You came onto him?" Anna said.

"It was kind of a mutual thing," Cleo said.

"That's retarded," Gwen said. Whenever they got together their vocabularies suffered.

"I told him he should pay me," Cleo said. "Just so, you know, he wouldn't feel bad."

Anna looked at her.

"Seriously," Cleo said.

It was as if they'd all counted to three together.

"He paid you," Anna said.

From downstairs came the distant clanking of pans. Daphne's father got up every morning at five and made breakfast for his wife. Soon they would smell coffee and toast.

"It wasn't about the money," Cleo said.

"Where is he now?" Anna asked.

"At the carriage barn, I guess," Cleo said. "He seemed kind of worn out."

"Oh, Cleo," Anna said.

"'Oh, Cleo,'" Cleo mimicked. "Get over yourselves," she said. "It's not like she's gonna *know*."

Gwen's anger had left. She sat in front of Cleo and held her friend's face in her hands. "What're you doing?" she asked.

Cleo took Gwen's hands and brought them down to the rug. "What're *you* doing?" she asked.

"Who cares what she knows," Gwen said. "*You* know."

"And so do you," Cleo answered. "And you, and you, and you," she said to the rest of them. She was doing Debbie Reynolds from *Singin' in the Rain*, but if they got that, they didn't respond.

"Hey," Gwen said, "I wasn't out in the playground."

"That's right," Cleo said. "*You* guys didn't do anything." A silence followed.

The truth was, she had run into Jack by accident— both of them insomniac and anxious—and she had come on to him, but it hadn't worked. They'd sat in the tree house and started to talk, but then they'd stopped and just sat there. She'd fallen asleep, and when she woke he was gone. The money was a lie. She didn't know why she said that kind of stuff.

"He said Daphne's friends were his friends. He said we could count on him for help whenever we needed it."

"He did not say that," Ticien said.

"Well, he implied it," Cleo said.

"Implied it how?" Anna said, the weary lawyer.

"You get an ear for these things after a while," Cleo said. "Well, at least I do," she added.

"Who gets an ear for what things?" Daphne asked from the doorway.

No one had heard her come in. After they recovered they registered her the way they always did, with a mix of pleasure and shame. They always spent so much time talking about her that when actually faced with her, they were surprised to rediscover the lift she gave them.

Anna stood and hugged her. "We're your ladies in waiting, planning what's to become of the rest of your day."

"Sounds ominous," Daphne said. She came over to them and sat on the floor. She tilted her head back and started to cry.

A charge darted among them all—it occurred to them that she might know—and they gathered around her like birds at a feeder. One held her shoulder, one rubbed her shin. One smoothed her hair off her face. She had tiny hands and large brown eyes. When she cried, they understood what she must've looked like at ten. They waited.

She took some breaths. "He's good, right?" she said, still crying. "You like him, right?"

They relaxed, understanding this wasn't about them.

"Why are you crying?" Gwen asked, since everything had a solution and you just had to identify the problem.

Ticien rolled her eyes. "She's sad, you moron."

"Daphne?" Gwen prompted.

Ticien took Gwen's chin and turned it toward her. "Stop ignoring me," she said.

Gwen took Ticien's hand and pulled it away before turning back to Daphne. "What are you most worried about?" she asked.

It turned out Daphne was worried about everything. Her father. He'd made Jack sign a prenuptial agreement. (Cleo already knew. Daphne's father had told her by the pool the day they'd arrived. "At least there's that," he'd said grimly, watching his daughter swim. At the playground Cleo had asked Jack about it. He'd been understanding.) Also, Jack's kids weren't coming to the wedding because Daphne had never even met them. He didn't want to push.

"You've never *met* them?" Anna said, and then after a moment, apologized.

Daphne swiped at her face. "Maybe it's too hard," she said, meaning the whole thing.

Gwen said, "You want us to tell you if you're doing the right thing." She was using her why-am-I-always-ahead-of-the-crowd voice.

Daphne was crying harder, confusing perception with kindness.

"Oh, sweetie," Anna said, rubbing her friend's shoulder. "We can't tell you that."

"Why not?" Daphne asked through her tears.

Gwen said, "It doesn't matter what we think; it matters what you think," and the rest of the girls nodded. They sat back, their work here done.

"Oh, please," Daphne said. She stopped crying. "Are you my friends or not?"

Her question didn't seem to be rhetorical, but nobody answered. She was not behaving as expected.

"Hello?" she asked.

She stood, the rest of them spread around her like shrubbery. "Here's what I'm telling you: I'm scared I'm making a mistake. I need to know what you *think*."

Downstairs the dog was barking. Her mother called for her father.

"I will call this wedding off," she said. "If I need to, I will."

Her ferocity finally wilted slightly, as if dampened by its own humid heat. "I make mistakes. That's what I do," she said.

No one answered, but they all thought of Charlie. He'd been the worst of all the cars she'd gotten into.

Her mother called again from downstairs to ask if one of them could please take the dog out; he was driving her crazy. And everyone had to eat breakfast. It was going to be a long day.

Her father opened the door. "Up and at 'em," he said, and scanned the scene. "What're you girls up to?" he asked.

Having known them since they were barely adults, and having never been privy to the unhappinesses they'd caused his daughter, he liked them. Even *had* he been privy to what they'd done, he might've still liked them, blaming, as he usually did, his daughter for her own sorrows. He was a Greek immigrant and a self-made millionaire. He believed you were responsible for your own successes and failures.

"Wouldn't *you* like to know," Cleo said. "This is girls only."

The summer after freshman year, visiting New York City, she'd seen him walking down First Avenue with his arm around a woman who was not his wife. He'd seen her see him. The incident allowed her certain latitudes.

"All right then," he said. "But even girls have to eat breakfast. I have my orders." With a last smile, he was gone.

"I'm asking for your help," Daphne said. "It's not very complicated," she added, and then she left.

It had never been clear what Charlie had done to her. The graduation plan had been to go to Anna's family's place on Nantucket for Dead Week—the days between final exams and graduation—but then according to Daphne's advisor, her thesis wasn't going to make the cut unless she stuck around to do some major work. She'd assumed the girls would go without her, and it had been a good assumption. No one would be able to say whose idea it had been, but somehow they all agreed to stay on campus. Daphne could work during the day and they'd play all night. It would be better than Nantucket. When they told her, Daphne's face colored in endearing ways, and whatever misgivings they'd had about changing their plans dissolved into the warmth of their status as Lady Bountifuls.

The campus had been mostly empty and unfamiliar, as if they'd all stepped into some kind of children's book, the town's twin discovered behind some high shrubs and rosebushes. Their dorm was deserted except for their suite of five singles, with one bath and a common room. Charlie was the kind of townie who made forays behind the college walls, and he and Daphne had been sleeping together for a while, so no one thought much of the sounds coming through the walls that last night of Dead Week.

It had been cool for the end of May and their windows were closed. But Daphne's room was in the middle, across from the suite's entrance, and they had heard others arrive. They wouldn't have been able to say for sure who they were. It had been a group, they knew that; maybe three.

They hadn't been able to hear everything, but they'd heard enough. They'd listened from their futon mattresses beneath childhood comforters surrounded by stuffed animals and photo collages of good times, and all the sounds they'd heard might not have been sounds of distress. Some of them still told themselves that.

And they'd all thought of the phone in the common room and getting help. But that would have required passing Daphne's door. They'd all listened and tried to gauge the number of people in her room. Maybe she was okay with whatever was going on in there. And would all five of them be enough to do anything if she wasn't? What if it wasn't even Charlie? If things got worse, they'd intervene. Some closed their eyes. Some stared out windows. Some held their breath. They were twenty or twenty-one. They were somebody's children, ashamed and afraid.

What haunted them most later that night and the next day and the day after, when it became clear that all Daphne was going to say was that Charlie and his friends had gotten weird on her, was the way she had quieted. They'd heard belt buckles on the floor and the thump of shoes. They'd heard boy sounds, muffled, but at some point they'd stopped hearing anything at all from Daphne. And none of them had asked that next day which friends, or just how weird.

And now she wanted something from them. They gathered after breakfast at the pool, its surface quiet and smooth in the morning light. The chairs were still damp with dew, and they sat on the slate instead, which was warmer and drier.

Across the lawn the band was running sound checks, and the caterers were setting up tables under the vast tent: wedding people doing their wedding things.

Cleo said, "What're we even talking about? She already knows what we think. We weren't exactly a chorus of reassurance when she asked what we thought of him. I mean, what do we think can happen here?"

Anna told her that that wasn't the point.

Gwen said that it was the point. "Okay, so we tell her we have major reservations. We give her some evidence for those reservations." She glanced at Cleo. "We have major reservations, right Cleo?" Gwen asked.

Cleo thought about the variety of reassurances she could offer. She gave Gwen a slow, middle-fingered wave.

Gwen turned away and went on, "And then what? She doesn't marry him, and we feel shitty. Or she does, and we feel shitty."

Anna said, "I already feel shitty."

Gwen said, "Or we tell her all the things we like about him, we leave out the major reservations, and then what? She marries him and she knows we lied to her. She marries him and blames us for years of unhappiness."

Cleo said, "She already seems pretty unhappy."

They were quiet.

"Maybe she marries him and they're happy," Anna said.

An already orange maple leaf drifted around the pool.

"Maybe," Cleo said. She sounded as if she was considering it.

Ticien, clear-eyed and calm after orange juice and muffins, said, "It's not about what she does with what we tell her; it's about us caring enough to speak up at all."

Gwen nodded, but Anna looked as if it was too late in the game.

Ticien, of all people, said, "Are you telling me we're too pathetic to do even that?"

The sun was over the trees. The sound of silverware and glasses carried across the lawn.

"What're you saying?" Gwen asked. "We tell her everything? The playground? Cleo?" She looked at them. "Everything?"

"Hey, Ms. Truth Detector," Cleo said. "I'm a symptom, not the original sin."

The girls were quiet, imagining Daphne's childhood bedroom with its Shaker furniture and handloomed rug. If they were telling her everything, they imagined how far back they'd have to go. They imagined the pain all around. And they all understood that they would list

Jack's qualities and strengths, the ways in which he was a good match, and hate themselves while they did it. And they understood that afterward they wouldn't be gathering again anytime soon. Life, they'd tell themselves, had gotten away from them. Because it was one thing to have a secret shame, and it was another to have to confess to yourself that you were never going to face it.

But they came together one last time, a year later. Their ten-year college reunion, not something Daphne had wanted to go to, but the divorce proceedings were under way and what else could she do with herself? Jack was living with ex-wife number five, whom he now had to admit he'd never stopped loving. He was paying Daphne a monthly settlement and had promised to resist his children's pressure to write her out of the will. None of the other girls were any closer to marriage, and the news of the split had been met with a mix of wariness and sadness. So okay, they thought, things would just be as they were.

"It's a road trip!" Cleo had effused at the rental agency, insisting on a minivan.

Topping the last hill, the college appearing below them, Daphne pressed her forehead to the window. "God, I hated this place," she said.

"No, you didn't," Gwen said.

Daphne didn't argue, but even they could see how miserable she was.

She suffered through the alumni parade, refusing to blow the kazoos. She drank and talked so much through the alumni achievement presentation that one of the class officers came up to their table to reason with her. "Did I sleep with this guy?" she asked Cleo as he pulled his chair closer. She seemed interested. "More than likely," Cleo answered. When Daphne laughed, the guy left.

It was, in other words, the ideal reunion. There was even a cameo by perfect Nancy Flanagan, who came up to Daphne at the kickoff keg and said she was glad to see she hadn't changed a bit. Daphne looked at her and then said, "Oh, now I remember you," before turning back to the bar.

The girls spent much of the weekend like long-married couples, scattered and socializing with everyone but each other, but last call at the bar after the after party the last night of the weekend found them squeezed into a red vinyl booth too small for the five of them, ordering final rounds of tequila shots. They were filled with the goodwill of people on the verge of a long-lasting separation and the self-congratulatory kindness of near strangers.

Around them, people were paying their bills. On the other side of the bar's picture window, their classmates lingered, their sundresses and blazers in mild disarray, putting off the end of something. They'd spent the weekend trying to suggest happiness and success and fulfillment and were tired, but they remained on the sidewalk, rocking side to side, growing chilly in the night air. Ahead of them were hotel rooms with spouses and sleeping children. They stood there, blinking and laughing, their hands falling onto the arms or shoulders of old friends and old lovers. Stay, they were thinking.

And then Charlie appeared, smiling and laughing as if he belonged, and the girls, like cats who'd been waiting outside a mousehole for days, thought, Oh, *there* he is.

Without thinking, Ticien said, "There's Charlie," and the girls snapped to. No one looked at Daphne.

Charlie pushed at one of the women's shoulders and gestured at her date, saying something the girls couldn't hear.

"He's gotten old," Cleo said.

He turned toward the window as if he'd heard, and they vaguely remembered the thrill of his attentions, but it all seemed like weather on the other side of the world, and he turned back around without noticing them. Daphne was pushing her empty shot glass around with a finger and seemed as if she might be able to make it through this. Pretending, you could manage a lot.

Charlie reached out and flicked the woman's hair. "How does he even *know* her?" Anna asked.

Not long after he and Daphne had started dating, the other girls had run into Charlie at this same bar. He'd wanted them to know he liked Daphne, really liked her. He hadn't been drunk. For a while they sat and listened. Then Gwen cleared her throat and suggested that Daphne might be kind of out of his reach, and the others added nothing but silence. His humiliation and rage had seeped into the room like floodwater. He stood there, his fists in his pockets moving beneath the fabric like animals. And then he left.

"That party at his buddy's place," Ticien said. "The night before graduation. He was all over her, remember?"

"The night before *graduation*?" Daphne asked. "The night after Dead Week?"

No one spoke.

"You're telling me you partied with those guys the night *after*?" she said.

It was as if something heavy and uneven had been rolled down a flight of stairs. It took a while for it to reach the bottom, the girls tracking its progress helplessly.

"After what they did to me?" she said. Her face was terrible to see.

"I don't remember that," Gwen said.

They were silent. "What *do* you remember?" Daphne asked.

Outside, the crowd had broken up, the street empty. Inside, everyone was right where they'd been.

"We all remember," Anna finally said. Daphne was still looking at them. She stood.

"We should go," Ticien said.

But it was as if that were Daphne's call.

"We still think about that night," Anna added.

"You still *think* about that night?" Daphne asked. "Well. *I* think about it, too."

They thought they'd been the drivers, but the truth was, she'd always been the car *they'd* chosen to get into. Where would they go without her?

But Daphne had given up on them. "I think about every *part* of that night," she said. And then she left, and none of them followed.

At some point in the years to come, each of them in their own genuine and inadequate ways would try to explain what they'd done. Anna would tell her husband that they'd been scared. Gwen would mutter to herself in the mirror. Ticien would tell her teenaged daughter that Daphne was the one who started everything, and they just followed. Cleo would call Jack, a month after the reunion, meet him for coffee, and tell him everything she remembered from that night in the suite. She would apologize for it. He would stare at her and tell her that of course she knew she was talking to the wrong person, right? Why did girls do these things to each other?

And Cleo, surprising herself, said because that's what girls do. They do stupid and hurtful things until they figure out not to.

And his expression was filled with the kindness of a parent. It was the closest thing to forgiveness any of them would receive.

. . .

The night of the wedding had been stunning. Everyone said so. White tents lit with white lights. Weather that made people laugh and shake their heads. All the sparkling people in their sparkling clothes.

It hadn't been about the walk down the aisle, or the first kiss, or everyone holding their peace. There had been no throwing of the garter, no dollar dance, no horseplay with the cake. Gwen had given a toast. Anna had read a poem. Cleo had done her pole dance, more acrobatic than exotic, to hooting and applause. And at the top of the night, as everyone's happiness was cresting, their fear like small sleeping animals outside the warmth of the campfire, the bridesmaids took the stage to belt out their signature song in their best sultry sister voices, starting out low and slow and then rising up and out of the tent and spreading across the lawn. *Gonna use my arms / Gonna use my legs.* The Pretenders! This was for one of their own, and they were a force to be reckoned with. For the final chorus, they pulled Daphne up front with them. *'Cause I gonna make you see / There's nobody else here / No one like me.*

They held each other and dipped and rolled. They turned their faces to the sky and waited for all that was theirs and all that was coming to them, and they couldn't have been happier.

JERKS

THE MAN I LOVE NOW WANTS TO KNOW IF I'VE EVER GONE out with someone as smart as I am.

We've got a whole weekend together and have spent most of it in bed, and we've just started talking about the other men. The army from my past.

Sure, I tell him: David was smart about cars. Maury knew about architecture. Putnam, he could train horses. I tell him I could go on and on.

"No, don't," he says, and pulls me to him.

In fifth grade, Peter Deckoff, who was big enough to be in eighth grade, pushed me through a doorway and told me to "get out of the way, you Chinese piece of junk."

He was being funny. The teacher made him stand in one of those jumbo-size garbage cans for an hour. It was a very progressive school. Teachers went by their first names.

I didn't try to help him explain, though I remember thinking that in China, junks are boats. I got the joke.

When I got to eighth grade, I danced with Greg Sullivan. This was at the "More Than a Feeling" dance. He was the only one taller than I was. He was embarrassed about his height and stood with hunched shoulders, so I often seemed taller anyway. I refused to hunch, though it would have made us both feel better.

We danced to "Stairway to Heaven" and "Two Out of Three Ain't Bad." We danced to "Summer Breeze." He moved me in a circle. His hands on my back left damp spots, and he smelled of oiled wood, and during the last dance he pulled back to look at me and said that I was pretty in an ugly kind of way.

Matthew and Craig, they were roommates in college. Craig was sophomore year. Matthew was junior. I stayed friends with both of them. Senior year, leaving a note for Matthew on his desk, I saw an envelope. A letter from Craig. Written across the back flap, like some sort of seal: *So, who's she sleeping with now?*

* * *

My senior year in high school, my best friend, a fairly unstable girl named Kristen, had a screaming fight with Ben, my first real love. I was a spectator. It was outside our high school after some sort of talent show.

She yelled all kinds of things. It was high school. Finally my boyfriend came up with a comeback.

"Cunt," he said. I was standing next to him.

She slapped him. I looked at his cheek. His skin was beginning to pinken, and I reached my hand to my own face, a gesture I still can't explain.

She left, and I stayed with him.

I walked him home. I put my hand on his shoulder and told him not to be upset; she was really angry with *me. I* was upset. That I didn't say. Instead I hooked his arm with mine and racked my brain for whatever subterranean thing I'd missed that could have made him say what he had. I had the impression he'd already put it out of his mind. It really, I remember saying, had nothing to do with him.

I broke up with Scott over the phone the summer between my second and third years of graduate school. He'd called the night before, telling me he'd tried to reach me all weekend. He'd gone to a party and had wished I was there with him. He had felt left out. There were so many couples.

In the morning I told him it wasn't fair of me to be with him. I loved him as a friend, but I wasn't in love with him. I thought I could've been (this was a lie), but I was wrong.

Yeah, he said. Yeah. He had been thinking the same thing.

We talked about other things. His family. My dog.

"So," he said after a pause, "we're gonna tell people it was mutual?"

The problem is that the man I'm in love with now—a man who I'm convinced is different—is married. A good man doing a bad thing. And how is that so different?

Chester the Molester: The artist who was from New Jersey and pretended that meant New York. He prowled the Houston art community. He prided himself on his nails. We were at a bar, actually in the parking lot of a bar, waiting for others. I don't know how he ended up in the group. We were leaning against a car. I was feeling sick. It was late. I'd been drinking. I'd just thrown up in the ladies' room. He didn't know that.

"Hey," he said. "I have a surprise for you."

I turned to look. "Yeah, what?"

He said, "This," and then he kissed me.

"God," I said. "Don't do that." My mouth was tight.

He held my chin between thumb and forefinger. "Mmm," he said. "Why not?"

There was a student-faculty lunch to discuss the future of the graduate program. Twelve of us sat around a circular table. The Eastern European poetry professor who had drifted in late debated aloud whether to sit next to his colleague or me, the second-year graduate student.

He said to his colleague in his slow, deliberate way that he was sorry, he liked him, but I was so much cuter, no?

I held my hand to my chest. I looked at the others and said, "Well. My goodness."

Later we had to squeeze together to make room for more latecomers. Someone asked the professor to move down still more, and he looked at me and said to the rest of the table, "It's a good direction, no?"

There were only a few chuckles. There were already rumors. The rumors were untrue. The truth—that I'd done little or nothing to squash the rumors, being somewhat flattered, and wondering idly if they could be put to any use—was worse.

There was another poet. A man I went out to drinks with a month after I broke up with my five-year lover. I let him kiss me. I had been pinching myself for a month; I wanted someone else to do it for me.

We kissed and kissed on my living room couch. "Why is it," he asked, propping himself above me, "that I have all my clothes on and you don't?"

My dress was unbuttoned. My bra was pushed aside. "I have my clothes on," I assured him.

Weeks later, after I told him I didn't think we were a good idea, he told me that if he'd pushed just a little bit more, we would've slept together, he could've convinced me.

"Oh, really?" I said.

He nodded. He had told our friends this.

He told our friends what?

A near miss. He'd told our friends it was a near miss.

I had wondered why a few days earlier a girl I knew had made a skimming motion, palm past palm, when she passed me in the student lounge.

The spring of my freshman year in college, Ben, my high school boyfriend, and I met in New York. We had a weekend of tears and decided to break it off.

I got back to school late Sunday night. There was a keg party outside my dorm. A senior hockey player blocked my way to the door. His teammates called him Mega.

"So," he said. "Hear you left something in New York."

I said news traveled fast.

He said he'd be interested in, you know, seeing me sometime.

"Sure, sure," I said. I just wanted to get through that door.

At the end of my graduate career I walked with the Eastern European poet and some friends across campus. He asked what I was going to do after school. I told him I wasn't sure.

"You could," he said, "come to Paris. You could be my secretary. My assistant."

My friends kept their eyes forward.

"Of course," he said, "I will have to check with my wife. I think as long as we don't show her a picture of you, we'll be fine, yes?"

My friends laughed and looked at each other.

Who, he wanted to know, would they find in the program to replace me?

My friends' expressions were poised between what I liked to read as jealousy and a wry disbelief at his comic persistence. I returned their looks and said, "Replace *me*? Is that possible?"

Gary was a senior when I was a freshman. He was an econ major. Bank of Boston after graduation. Boston, he told me, wasn't all that far from school. He could visit all the time. He'd be coming back to see friends anyway.

With Matthew, the first of the roommates, it started during summer break. In someone's cabin in Maine. Four of us in bed after a beach cookout and a late-night swim. We closed our eyes and kissed. I closed my eyes, thinking that protected me. His brother, my girlfriend, and a random partygoer all slept next to us, and I thought: *Don't talk. Don't say anything yet. Let's just kiss.*

Matthew reminded me of Teddy Moss from high school. Teddy, who never studied and got double 800s on his SATs. Teddy, who played lacrosse and skimmed his ten-speed across New York City streets.

Matthew looked just like him. I never got Teddy.

The man who lasted five years moved to Texas with me only because he had to. I was going to school there and he could, I pointed out, do what he was doing anywhere. He was the one who knew about horses. He couldn't think of any arguments in time. For my birthday, three months after we moved, he gave me a subscription to *People.*

The near-miss poet, on our first date, before any kissing at all, told me he'd been warned about me.

By whom? I wanted to know.

He didn't want to say. But they had told him he should watch out. That I toyed with men.

They? I thought.

...

Bob I met at my first job after graduate school. A writer: articles in local newspapers and magazines. Novels, unpublished, in his filing cabinet drawers. A story in the *New Yorker* that I heard about way before I met him.

He was married. During a fight, his wife told him that his problem was he was in love with me. He told her she was right.

This he told me outside my house, on my stoop.

"Oh, Bob," I said, getting up, brushing off the backs of my pants. "You don't love me. You just think you do."

Sitting very still, with his hands spread over his thighs, he wanted to know what the difference was.

The man I love now says, "When you told me about Bob before, you didn't say he was married."

I lean closer to find his mouth. I part my lips to meet his. I keep my eyes open, as if checking for similarities.

Here's one big difference: the man I love now has already gone out on a limb. He told his wife, not the other way around; they started counseling. But here's the problem: the man I admire wouldn't be doing this.

Putnam, my five-year lover, gave me for college graduation a silver bracelet engraved with elephants. It would've been *really* great, but he had no way of knowing how much I love elephants.

I hugged him and told him I loved him. First time. We had already established that he had never told anyone that. I had sworn to myself that I wouldn't say it first.

Chin on my shoulder, he said, "I love you too, I guess."

I registered the "I guess," but I also thought, tallying up the score: *No one else. The only one.*

Once told that he didn't really love me, Bob the married writer wrote a story about me. My hair became red. My eyes green. His woman didn't have a hand. That, he wrote, was the thing he loved most about her.

The copy he gave me had *for your eyes only* written across the first page in purple felt-tip. The sentence was cornered with stars, and finished with exclamation point, exclamation point.

A few months after his Chinese junk wisecrack, I sat behind Peter Deckoff during meeting time. He was picking at something on his neck. It was a tick. I watched him pull it out. He looked at it, then behind him, at me. I said, loudly, matter-of-factly, "Peter just pulled a tick out of his head."

It took the student teacher five minutes to calm everyone down. She pinned the tick to a small square of Styrofoam, hoping to transform this into a science lesson.

Classmates kept an eye on me while she talked. I pantomimed how he had pulled the tick out. Then they took him in, sitting now at a table of his own. Everyone had made a stink about sitting near him. When he looked over at me, I pointed at his neck.

Putnam and I went to Vero Beach for vacation. We met some friends for beer and oysters at a restaurant on the shore. We sat at grayed picnic tables, shivering in the beach wind.

He carved something in the table. He always carried a Buck knife in his front jeans pocket and a small sharpening stone in the change pocket. I glanced at what he was working on. His name. He had *P-U-T* so far.

As we got up to leave, he turned to me and said, "See, now we'll be here forever."

"We" and "forever" didn't often come out of his mouth in the same sentence. He had my attention.

He'd carved his name and my initials. The two were connected by a plus sign. His name, and my initials? *Exactly*, I thought. *Equals what?*

"Yeah," I said, burying my nose in his neck. "Forever."

Craig was the romantic who never tired of pointing that out. He left jelly beans on my desk in the library. He called attention to the beauty of sunsets, spectacular or otherwise. He always wanted to play his guitar and sing a song. James Taylor. "Fire and Rain."

Putnam and I drove across Texas east to west. Acres of flatness, desert, and wire fencing. Cattle and rabbits, armadillos and birds. I sat in the car, taking in the view out my window, thinking: This is good. This is right.

A solitary cow raised her head to inspect us as we drove by. Putnam looked back at the animal in our rearview mirror and said, "It's like she's going, 'Fellas? Hey, fellas? Where'd everybody go?'"

I laughed. A real laugh.

That was nice. That laugh, I mean.

I stood by Craig's bed, bending at the waist to get something out of my bag. He lay on his side, propped on his elbow. "Hey," he said. "Looking good in those jeans, babe." He reached forward and ran a hand down the leg closest to him.

The first one—lover? jerk?—was ten years older. I was sixteen. My girlfriend and I met him at the same time. Some club downtown that we weren't supposed to be at. He was introduced to her and took her hand to kiss. She threw her head back and laughed. I was next. I held out mine. He smiled crookedly, elbowed his buddy, and when he leaned over, I could feel the shape of his smile on the back of my hand.

Later that night, when he was on top of me in his buddy's bed, he held my arms over my head, both wrists in one hand, and told me I hadn't seen anything yet.

When my high school boyfriend and I broke up, he warned me about getting involved with other guys too quickly. He wanted me to remember the reputation I had before I started going out with him. Our relationship had fixed that. I wouldn't want to go and ruin everything now, would I?

"No," I said.

"Thanks," I said, and slept with a guy everyone knew was a jerk.

Once Putnam and I were watching TV and I saw the guy with the crooked smile in a Lysol ad, welcoming country fresh into his life.

"Hey," I said, pointing. "That's Jack."

Putnam looked.

"The guy I lost my virginity to," I said.

"Oh great," Putnam said, stretching out. "Now I've gotta worry about some guy on TV?"

. . .

Senior year of college, a girlfriend from home came to visit. I gave her a tour of the campus, and we ran into Scott.

He wanted to know if I was pointing out all the locations of my conquests.

I smiled too broadly. "No," I said, "that isn't the tour we're on."

"Yeah," he said, smiling. "That would take way too long."

In ninth grade, Adam Mirtz and Susan Blair went out. She went away for the weekend. I sat next to Adam on someone else's couch and laughed at things he said, made the kind of comments that always made boys say, "She's like one of us," and worked my hand between his leg and the cushion, moving my fingers slowly back and forth against his corduroy.

The man I'm in love with now: I know his wife. I've eaten dinners she's prepared. I've talked with her about the plans she has for their house. I've helped her tease her husband.

It would kill me, if I found out my husband was having an affair, to realize I had made dinner for the woman. I had laid out towels.

That Tuesday Adam Mirtz said *Let's just be friends* to Susan Blair.

That next Saturday we squished next to each other on my single bed and watched hours of free HBO. One of those promotional weekends.

We kissed. He had red hair and freckles. His mouth was small and smelled stale and old.

Sunday night I called to tell him I was sorry, I didn't think it was going to work. Maybe, I suggested, it wasn't too late to talk to Susan again?

These stories have a complicated relation to the man I love now. Telling him these stories is complicated. He knows both of these things. There's a lot of intimacy here. And aggression. It's a long warning that he has already acknowledged he understands.

He's had two other affairs. He says those were different, and I believe him, but what do I know? He says those were secret, and this one is not. He didn't leave his wife for those women.

He hasn't left her for me.

Bob the married writer left the job before I did, with a teaching appointment, a contract for his first novel, and a rejuvenated marriage.

The following spring, I got a postcard. It was handwritten. It said:

> Recent publications by Bob Hansen: August 1992, "The Shark Pool," the *New Yorker*. September 1992, "Eyes as Blue as Mine," the *Atlantic*. March 1993, "The One-Handed Girl," the *Paris Review*.

. . .

And what about Gino LaBruna? Gino LaBruna only had relatives named Anthony or Maria Teresa. All the men were dentists.

He was fooling around with my best friend in high school, the unstable one. Nothing serious, he told me. He was walking me home one afternoon. He kissed me outside my apartment building.

"I know," I said and kissed him back, thinking of what she had said about his mouth.

He had told my best friend that I had beautiful legs. People never said stuff like that. It was nice, standing there, in front of him, in the vee of his legs, watching his hands on my thighs, knowing that his liking my legs meant he liked me.

No one, the man I'm in love with now tells me, has loved your body like I love your body.

And I believe him.

When Bob the married writer told me he loved me, what else could I say but *No, you don't?* The second his words hit the air, he was gone. I had him. He was nothing.

John was the summer after freshman year. I met him at Willie's or the West End after I got off my waitressing shift, my pockets filled with ones and fives. He drank too much. He was always pushing his dirty hair out of his eyes. He talked about driving his MG convertible down

California coast roads. He told me that when he rode his motorcycle, he never wore a helmet.

He asked me, toward the end of the summer, what I would do if, say, I went abroad for a semester and fell completely in love with someone. Would I, like, stay in the foreign country?

His leg bounced under the table while he asked.

I told him that first of all, I wouldn't fall in love with anyone that quickly. But if I did? "Big if," I said. "But if I did, I'd go back to school." I picked up my beer and looked at him. "Why?" I asked. "What would you do?"

He told me he'd stay; if he was in love, he'd stay.

I told him he could never be sure. It was too easy, I knew, to convince yourself of anything.

I was more in love with Matthew's mom than with Matthew. She was dying of cancer when we started going out my junior year in college. She wore scarves to hide the neck brace, men's sweaters for the back one. She stopped wearing her wedding ring because she never knew how much swelling the drugs were going to cause.

She loved books. She'd been a seventh-grade teacher. She loved making things. She knitted sweaters. She painted. She cared about her children: Matthew and his brother. I visited them at their farmhouse in Pennsylvania. She couldn't keep from them. Her hands strayed to theirs at meals. She took the long way around a room to pass them and touch their shoulders, the backs of their necks. Her bunnies, she called them.

When she died, Matthew and I hadn't been a couple for two years. I was living with Putnam. Matthew called to tell me, give me the details. The family had gone to the hospital. They had all gotten to talk with her. She had squeezed his hand.

That had been in June. He called in August. He had been talking to Craig the Romantic. Craig had suggested that I might want to hear.

I hated Matthew for this. Absolute hate. No chance for forgiveness.

John and I ended up in his bed, naked and a little drunk. He pushed my legs open wider with his knee. I asked what he was doing.

"Well," he said. "You tell me. It's your call."

Five years after Matthew's mother died, I saw him at Craig's wedding. The few of us who knew each other from college stayed up until four in the morning the night before the wedding. We snuck into the hotel hot tubs, balancing glasses of wine and whiskey on the slippery tile edges of the tubs. Matthew's legs found my waist in the hot, churning water, and even before everyone else left, he had me wrapped to him, my hands on his shoulders.

In other words, five years after he had done something I had announced to myself to be unforgivable, I pulled off my wet bathing suit for him, in a public place, wedged myself into a corner of a hot tub, and, already feeling hungover, let him think he had no reason to treat me any differently. And in fact, he *had* no reason to treat me any differently.

"That was fun," he said, the next morning. We were standing around in our wedding clothes. I deserved it.

After Ben and I slept together for the first time, he told me that he wished I hadn't slept with anyone before him. Before I could begin to reassure him, he said, "Because, you know, I was so nervous. I mean, you have all that experience."

A long-ago one-night stand calls during the second night of our weekend. The man I love doesn't get out of bed. I hold his hand throughout the conversation. The long-ago one-night stand is upset about the way his life is going. His divorce, his girlfriend, his job. I have trouble cutting it short.

I hang up. Things are awkward. Eventually the man I love tells me this is not how he expected the night to go. It turns out it was pretty hard to listen to me.

"I'm sorry," I say. I take a breath to say it again. This would've been my usual pattern. It suddenly seems important not to keep to that pattern. "Hey," I say, surprising myself. "Let's remember who's married here."

That first man: I couldn't sleep next to him, and my insides felt like nothing I knew. I got out of bed, sixteen years old, wrapped myself in a sheet that had wild animals all over it, went to lie on the couch across the room, and tried to remember what I used to feel like. Like when I had a cold and looked at all the healthy people around me, trying to remember what it felt like to be them.

Why do I think the man I love now might be different? The clearest way I can explain it is this: When we were first dating, Putnam, the five-year one, came to my room at four in the morning. It was the middle of winter and he was wearing a tweed jacket, the lining sneaking out from the sleeves. He was carrying an album, and he leaned down and told me he had something that I had to listen to. I just had to. He fumbled around in the dark with the stereo and then came to lie down behind me just as Patsy Cline started with "Walkin' after Midnight."

He held me, still wearing his jacket, touching me with as much of his body as he could, telling me, his mouth at my ear, that he'd been alone in his room, and he'd *known*, like in one sharp instant he'd known, all he wanted to do was hear *this* song, with me, that night.

The man I love now makes me feel like that a shocking amount of the time.

But the man I love now would also point out that the example I'm using comes from another relationship.

On Sunday afternoon, end of the weekend, I ask the man I'm in love with now whether he's going to leave his wife.

I want to tell him I'm not very good at this belief thing. I want to tell him I'm the sort of person who needs lots of evidence.

The thing is, I don't have to tell him any of this. He knows without me saying a thing. But when nothing happens and we're both silent, I think: *Won't his knowing and not acting be worse than his not knowing at all? Do we deserve happiness? Do we deserve what we'll get?*

After Craig's wedding, Matthew and I ended up at adjoining gates at the airport. We made small talk, and then when it was time to board we hugged and said how great it had been to see each other. He pulled back and kept his hands on my shoulders. He wanted, he said, to tell me something he had never told me before. "I love you," he said. "I never told you that when we were together." He looked down, then back up to my eyes. "Guess I didn't have the guts or something."

He was the same guy, and I had screwed him in a hot tub. That was the situation. Maybe it was him; maybe it was his mother. Either way a small hole inside of me was getting stretched until it seemed like the best way to describe me was to point out what was no longer there.

So I fixed my face, and put my hands on my forearms to steady myself, and tried something cosmopolitan. "Or," I said, "you just didn't love me then."

"Yeah," he said. "You're probably right." And it hit me that knowing how we had done this together wasn't going to make me feel any better.

So here I am, thirty-five years old, and they all haunt me. And I'm supposed to be head over heels. And the man I love now tells me he has to spend his life with me.

This is a cool breeze on a bus stuck in traffic. This is what I've waited months for. And still I'm standing here, short a reaction. He's waiting.

I'm willing to believe he admires me. I'm willing to believe he needs me around for the rest of his life. But do I want to keep performing? Do I want to keep doing what needs to be done? There are all these surprises. He surprises me. I surprise myself. But going home alone, stepping out of the ruins of those attachments: it was exhilarating. I could shut the door and be alone with myself. Which may have been the perfect punishment, the ultimate self-indulgence, the thing I loved the most.

THE MOTHERS

WE ARE THE MOTHERS. OUR NAMES ARE KIM, OR LINDA, OR Janice, or Sue. Sometimes Kristine, or Emilie, who grew up in Canada, but not Brittney or Ashlee with two *e*'s. We live in small New England towns known for their picturesque beauty, named after Native American tribes or founding fathers, ending in *ville* or *field*. Our houses are raised ranches or Capes or converted barns or former farmhouses. They're in neighborhoods with bike-friendly roads, walking distance to the elementary school and playground. Or at the end of modest dirt driveways in an open meadow with partial views. We drive minivans or SUVs with bike racks on the back and Thules on the roof. Sometimes a pickup, if we're Republican and borrowed our husbands' cars. (We're mostly Democrats, but avoid talking politics if we can. And religion, which most of us never had or have left behind, though some of us are still, shall we say, in the front pews.) Almost all of us are white.

We have camp chairs with drink holders and shade canopies in the trunks of our cars, along with cases of Gatorade, first aid kits filled with smack packs, Rubbermaid cupcake holders, and lasagna pans. If our husbands coach, also orange sports cones and milk crates filled with water bottles. Picnic blankets and golf umbrellas. Some of us are former athletes, and some still compete in half triathlons. Some of us take Pilates. Some walk vigorously twice a week with friends or the dog. Some of us work, some don't. We are all mothers. Some of us are naturally thin, some are not. All of us are competitive, and, in this way, like our sons. We're the mothers of girls as well. But when we think: *mother*, we do not think: *daughter*. We're not sure why this is. We love our daughters like she-wolves, but we think of ourselves as the mothers of boys.

These are our boys at four and then six and then twelve and fourteen. They've spent their lives together, in school, at home, and on the playing fields. They sleep over in basement playrooms ("man caves," we call them, semi-ironically) like a puppy pile of overfed giraffes, with candy wrappers and soda cans littered around them. One of them is on the laptop, several on their phones, two more on the Xbox. Some look twenty, some eleven. Some tower over their fathers, some are half the size. Some are shaving, some insist that they *need to*. Some still kiss us good-bye at the bus stop. Some tell us nothing. Some tell us everything. Some are angry. Some are sad. Some are happy, genuinely happy, and this makes our hearts fill to spilling. When they're sad, we think: *How can we fix this?*

They're a hall of mirrors in which we see ourselves, past, present, and future: secret hopes, genetic legacies, future possibilities. We love their limbs draped over furniture, their elephant tread above us upstairs, their inadequate fibs, their sudden and inexplicable questions at dinner, their attempts at humor.

They crawled together, ate the same lint off the same floors, learned their math facts, and watched the puberty video in a pack. They share clothes, eat each other's food, see the same movies, mock the same teachers. They use the same skin products (though some need them more than others), preen for the same amount of time in front of bathroom mirrors. They've played on the same teams: soccer, football, lacrosse, hockey, basketball. Their fathers tell them comic anecdotes about their own rebellious younger days. (One lit his bed on fire. One on a dare ate sand. One broke his arm jumping out of a neighbor's window.) Fathers.

Years were taken off our lives by their sports. Baseball almost killed us all. A metaphor for life: you do what you can to give them the rules and then send them out on the field, and a high fly ball heads right toward him, your boy, and you can do nothing but watch. And don't even talk to us about pitching.

Our hearts broke watching our boys. Our hearts lifted watching our boys. We sat on our hands as coaches or husbands yelled at our boys. (And they wonder what it is about mothers and boys. *Someone* has to balance the seesaw.) We've driven hours in silent, unhappy post-game cars. We've paid for hundreds of dollars' worth of celebratory soft-serve. Thousands for cleats. And equipment. And team sweatshirts, T-shirts, hats, and warm-ups. And concession-stand food. And 50/50 tickets. And those socks that *all the guys are wearing.* We've watched their small proud smiles as they jog in after coming up with the line drive for the third out. We've learned about hot corners, and two guards, and nickelbacks. We've had fourth graders sink the halftime buzzer-beaters, and their grins seek us out in the stands. We've come home after dropped flies in the bottom of the ninth and taken our husbands into the other room, held a finger up to their faces, and vehemently whispered, *Do something. This is your moment. Be a dad.*

We've dealt with sons told they won't be in the starting lineup and talked to coaches about it. And then told our boys: Just do better. Without always having kept the impatience out of our voices. We're the ones suffering the most, we've often thought. Why can't our boys help out? Quit backing away from the plate? Swing through? Why can't they just try harder? Be better?

And then there are the injuries. Concussions from slick gym floors. New sneakers. One boy slips, the sound of his head on the wood enough to penetrate the cacophony of gym acoustics. The ref gestures the other kids away (they all know to take a knee) and crouches near. The assistant coach, the boy's father, joins him. The boy's head to the side, as if he's listening to the floor. Mothers in the stands, trained not to run out onto the floor like hysterics. We don't talk to our boys on the bench or between innings. The father searches the stands with his eyes. The mothers lean forward. Come, he gestures, and the rest of us sink back, watching her make her careful way down the bleachers, thinking: *He's not moving* and *Thank God it's not my boy.*

Because this is what it means to be the mothers. You're a team of your own, ready to pull your weight, ready to play with pain, ready to leave it all on the field, but you're still on the sidelines waiting for someone else's end-to-end rush, or gunning from three, or taking on four defenders himself. It may be a team, but there are always standouts. One mother says she wants her son to look back and think: *I had the best mother ever.* The rest of us roll our eyes, exclaiming at her lunacy when she's not around. But let's not fool ourselves. If anyone's walking away with the lifetime achievement award, we know who it will be.

When the boys are fourteen and done with youth sports, they're ninth graders. It's the Monday after Thanksgiving, first day of basketball tryouts. There's a new coach. There will be cuts. These are not boys who want Division I scholarships, though they'll all tell you they're going to Carolina. One, maybe two, might be recruited by Division III programs. One says he'll play in the NBA and then be a famous writer. He asks his mother how many NBA players have gone on to be famous writers. Fewer than you'd think, she tells him, handing him his lunch.

These are boys who love high school sports. Even if they play in college, they tell us, they will never again play with a group of guys they've known since they were four. And this is basketball. They love the speed of it, the hyperbolic myths about which of them almost dunked. The sound of the ball going through the hoop, one boy tells his mother, is such a perfect sound the only thing that can describe it is the sound itself.

And so, now, every day after the three days of try-outs, we modulate our tones and avoid eye contact as we ask what our boys want for dinner and then, as an afterthought, How'd it go?

We worry. We engage in hushed conversations with our husbands late at night in bed. Our boys think of themselves as athletes and may be turning out to be less popular than they thought they'd be, less book smart, afflicted with worse skin, not as tall. What will happen if this, too, is taken from them? *How can we fix this?* we think even later at night, after our husbands fall into sleep, exhausted with us.

We carpool after tryouts and try not to let the boys know that we're mentally stacking them up against each other. This one plays the same position as that one. That one's slower but more aggressive. There are too many guards. If only he were big enough for small forward. We curse whatever's been in our town's water that has produced an abundance of boys. The girls'

team is out beating the bushes to get one set of varsity starters together, let alone a varsity and a JV, eleven
on each. But even hearing that, we're thankful to have
boys.

Our boys reassure us. Settle down, they say. I'm
working hard. I'll be fine. (We don't find this reassuring.
We've seen their version of working hard.)

Our boys worry us. What if I don't make it, they say
in darkened bedrooms, their childhood night-lights
glowing. I *love* basketball, they say. What if I don't make
it? They're near tears. And our hearts batter against their
cages while we keep our voices steady. You will, you will,
we say, over and over, like a lullaby. And we rub their
foreheads like we used to when they were tiny, and tuck
the blankets under their chins, and kiss them good-night,
and tell them not to worry, that we love them for who
they are, not what they do. We do what we can. And then
we fall into our own beds for another sleepless night.

In the morning, while the boys move around upstairs, dressing for school after being called four times,
we talk about it over coffee with husbands weary of the
conversation, weary of us, weary of our excessive love
for these boys. We trample the same ground. We hold
our cups with two hands and forget to pour one for our
husbands. We lay out waffles with Nutella for our boys
and call them a fifth time. We collapse our heads onto
our husbands' chests. Why can't we just give them this?
we ask. It's a rhetorical question. Our husbands stroke
our hair and rub circles on our backs. You can't protect

them from everything, they say. I know, we answer. *Why not?* we think. If they're not good enough for the team, they're not good enough, our husbands add. *And whose fault is that?* we think.

When we've been enraged with our boys, we've sometimes cursed at them and they've turned to us, eyes wide with mock disbelief. What kind of mother, they ask, talks to their kid that way? And sometimes, if we're really enraged, we go on: The kind who got up early to make your lunch and breakfast and to help you get your hair right and find your shirt. The kind who's done two loads of sweaty boy laundry before you're out the door. The kind who's argued with your teachers over grades, and helped you study for quizzes, and endlessly replaced lost sweatshirts and water bottles. And paid for tutoring and extra training and coaching sessions. The kind who's pushed and pulled and yanked you into the boy you are. And what have you contributed? What kind of boy won't meet a mother like that halfway? What kind won't see what we're going through? What kind has as his favorite thing to say to his mother: *What's wrong with you?* Or, even worse: *Get a life?* What kind of boy says *that* in the face of all we've given and all we've suffered?

And one of us—me—explains for the millionth time to my husband that I *know* our boy is not going to be playing in college, except in intramural pickup games, and I know he's not going to be playing *after* college, except in driveways with his own sons. I just want to give him *this*. High school basketball, for Chrissakes. JV. JV would be fine. The *bench* on JV would be fine. I *know* he's not that good.

But my boy is in the doorway, and the expression I've put on his face is something I'm not getting rid of.

Oh honey, I say. And I reach for him, but he ducks and makes his way past me to the table.

My husband fills his own cup of coffee and leaves us to each other. Because these are our boys, and we are the mothers, here to do what mothers do best.

A FINE LIFE

MY NAME IS CHOU YUAN, BUT HERE IN CENTRAL FLORIDA where I have lived for the last many years they know very little about me and not certainly how to pronounce my name, so in their mouths I come out sounding like a dog with desires. This is not something that bothers me. A dog with desires is not a bad thing to be, but when they call for me it always takes a minute to remember who it is they want. To keep people from thinking I am rude, which I am not, I begin many sentences with, "In my country." Almost always, with whatever it's paired, that explains enough.

In the area we call the playroom, quiet and calm are essential. The two mothers must sit low to the ground, become hills, rolls in the earth. Mothers must not look at the baboon to whom theirs is being introduced. One's hopes for this meeting must not be revealed. If all goes well, the bond will be lifelong, and will make all the difference for reintroduction to the natural habitat. The baboons who fail at this, their introduction to a group of two, will fail at everything. They will be here with us for life.

We mothers must pretend we are bored. We must fulfill monkey expectations of what it means to be human: simpleminded, like them at a slower speed.

Sally disapproves of calling them monkeys, but certain baboons are sometimes called Dog-Faced Monkey. A name from a Chinese fairy tale. In the early going, it made connection easier for me, and this was something that Sally could not object to.

Today is October 1, 2004. In my country, my people (another useful phrase) are celebrating the Communist victory of 1949. Today I am at the end of my forty-ninth year and can feel it in my stomach like sudden hunger. The auspiciousness of my birth date was compensation for my gender, my parents used to tell me. After my mother died, my father said not to worry; it was a small sacrifice for the good fortune of having a true revolutionary in the family. I was twelve; I had come home a newly anointed Young Pioneer, my bright red scarf around my skinny neck. I thought my father's tears were tears of pride until behind him I saw my aunts and uncles, gathered together in the middle of a workday.

I am told those scarves have now become something to collect. Another volunteer in this facility once asked if I had any souvenirs secreted away somewhere. *Souvenir* seemed like precisely the wrong word. I told her I didn't, my lie so easy it felt like truth. She said I was lucky to have gotten out. Sally heard her, but her hands stayed busy with boxes of formula on a shelf.

The girl had compared surviving 1975, before the fall of the Gang of Four, to surviving the last year of World War II in Auschwitz. She was a short, brown-haired girl with round spectacles. A history major, given to exaggeration. Sally once told her she was "a very lovely unspoiled girl."

Yes, I agreed. Very lucky. I didn't tell her luck had little to do with anything. In my country, whom you know and what you're willing to do or say is what counts. The length and breadth of your selfish desires. That's what we learned. But of course that was what the girl had meant: that was what her words had said beneath their surface.

So I am middle-aged, but my people age well. I have no gray hairs, just the wrinkles that suggest the terrain of my face in the years to come. The skin on the backs of my hands, when pinched by curious baboons, snaps back. Both sets of grandparents lived into their nineties. In my family, self-preservation was a point of pride.

Today I am introducing Zeus to Ripley. We name our infant charges. Something powerful, Sally instructs, a name that will see them through. I choose names from Greek mythology. Of which I knew nothing until Sally handed me a copy of *Bulfinch's Mythology* and said I might be interested. I was. Desires of extraordinary proportions: the gods' lives in that way seemed the stuff of ordinary life.

Exactly, Sally had responded, smiling.

Ripley was named by her foster mother, a young woman from Sweden with the torso of a tree trunk. The name is from a movie I have never seen.

Zeus came to us from an animal testing laboratory in the north. A watchdog agency had managed to save him. Still infant enough for black fur and pink skin, his eyes were hollow, his breathing raspy. One hand hung useless and sad. Our vet amputated it, put him on antibiotics, and it healed nicely—a perfect arm, missing a hand. In its place, a delicate pucker. He likes to have it scratched. His eyes fill with surprise, as if until your touch he hadn't known he had the itch.

Out of the fifteen volunteers, Sally assigned me as Zeus's mother. The timing was right—Athena, my previous charge, had graduated to one of our junior troops. Our most senior troop had just been released in a game park in South Africa.

I had time. Orphaned baboons cannot be placed individually in the wild; they must relearn their social dynamics here and go with the troop from our facility or not go at all. So some of it was timing, but I also like to think that by now Sally trusts me with the hard cases, the ones that if she were thirty years younger she would handle herself. After all, the other volunteers live here temporarily, in the bunkhouse. I am a permanent resident with my own trailer just across the central yard from Sally's. I don't have any real reason to think Sally favors me, but what harm does it do?

For the past eight weeks, Zeus has been with me, on my body, it seems, twenty-four hours a day. I have fashioned a sling out of a scarf, which leaves my hands free for the dawn-to-dusk chores we all have here. I have diapered him in the usual way—a hole for his tail, backward to keep his one hand from picking at the sticky tabs. He has slept in my bed, received his bottles, then some solids, allowing himself to be cradled and loved. And now he is clinging to my shirt, his old man's head burrowing into my armpit, keeping one eye on the female just his age in the opposite corner of the big cage. I am not supposed to merely turn him loose. I am supposed to be there if he needs me, but not supposed to let him think that what I really want is for him to stay in my armpit.

This is not hard for me. The moment when the babies jump from me: that is the moment that makes me feel as if I have taken flight.

It's a fine life. It was not one that I asked for, but it's a fine life.

I hear in Sally's voice the tone that I've come to understand means this is the sixth or seventh time she has called my name. I don't like to disappoint her. She is the kind of woman who has hope for us humans. She makes me want to be the person she thinks I am. I don't know how she ended up here. She is South African. Who knows what her secrets are. "I'm sorry," I tell her.

"There's someone here to see you," she says, gesturing behind her. With her, Zeus and Ripley forget their wariness and pin themselves against the cage to get close to her. She leans against it, letting her white hair be tugged and stroked. When she goes away for fund-raising, some of the monkeys won't eat until her return. Others climb the fake trees and lie on their backs, their toes wrapped around the ceiling wire.

She's not surprised that I have a visitor. In fifteen years, I have never had one, but she is the kind of woman who, if you pointed this out, would say, "Well, now she does." Last week, she came upon me crying in the nursery. She didn't ask any questions. She believes in the inevitability of tears. Normally, I find this part of her reassuring, but today I do not. I am almost angry. I want to tell her that in the twenty-five years I've lived in this country, I have never had a visitor. But she would tell me that I couldn't have lived here for twenty-five years without someone coming to my door. So I say nothing.

At first he looks like one of the crowd, his head softened by a short brush of gray hair. His ears are oversized. Zeus is back on me, curled in the crook of my arm. He regards the stranger. Of course, I have many times imagined this scene. And perhaps it is for this reason that I am strangely calm. He is remarkably unchanged, and I know the mole on his earlobe, the triple lines between his eyebrows, his broad, square mouth. He is excessively well dressed, and I allow myself to think that perhaps all we will have to face after twenty-five years is a little bit of aging and the awkwardness of reunion. It is a false thought.

Sally unlatches and relatches the outer door; waits at the inner one. "Go on, " she says. "Greta and I will take the babies for a walk."

At the sound of the door, Zeus springs from me.

"Father," I say, in Chinese, rising to my feet. "It's you."

At first I think this resembles one of those Chinese American movies the other volunteers always ask if I've seen. We sit on the bench under the palms outside my trailer home, speaking our language. Behind that, there are highway noises. We don't talk about our past. Or how we got where we are. In my country, one is never surprised by where one ends up. It's like living on ice floes in a heat wave.

We talk about the election. He is volunteering for the Democrats. He has come down from New York City to go door to door to get out the vote. He has pamphlets. We haven't seen each other in twenty-five years, I didn't even know he was in this country, and he wants to make sure I'm registered, that I have a ride to the polls. So maybe, I think, it is a different kind of movie.

I tell him I've never voted, though it has been my right for many years. He seems to ignore this. I look remarkably unlike him. It makes me feel more his daughter. My hands are around my cup of tea. Small lizards crawl on the rocks by my feet. Sally is in the playground, Zeus swinging above her, wild, one-arm loops around a high bar. He's screaming with delight. Every two or three turns, he stops and bobs his head in that gliding way at her. He waits for her applause and then is off again.

A volunteer delivers a plastic tub filled with bottles to the kindergarten troop. Another group of mothers washes and rinses the plastic containers we use to mix formula on the porch of Sally's double-wide. Sometimes they laugh.

Bill from the bakery lowers the tailgate of his flatbed, delivering the bread he donates. Sally gets no government subsidy and says she is totally dependent on the generosity of others. She says this as if it's something she wants us to be proud of. I am working on that. Bill is flirting with Sonya, the newest volunteer. We are all women here. It makes sense, I suppose. Who else would devote themselves to something like this?

My father tells me this is a strange place. I agree. We are quiet and then he returns to his pamphlets.

It will be more of the same, he says, if I don't vote for the right candidate.

I tell him that I wouldn't mind more of the same. More of the same will be fine with me.

He shakes his head and makes the same disapproving noises he made when I couldn't grasp my biology homework. It's the noise I use when disciplining the monkeys. "Have you learned nothing?" he asks. "Twenty-five years, and you still know so little? What was the point in your coming here at all?"

This is a good question. I was supposed to have returned by now: the loyal Young Pioneer, the model Red

Guard. There had been no reason to believe I wouldn't. And so use had been made of my father's connections. We went, as we say in my country, through the back door. I was to go to Boston, learn about nuclear physics, and come back to build a stronger China. Not to save the world, but to save our world. The plight of others has never been a central concern of my people. It doesn't make us bad. How do you think about others when you are in situations of such desperation? Do we owe others more than we owe ourselves?

I've spoken out loud apparently.

Father lifts the tote bag between his legs. "You owe only what you can offer," he says.

"I couldn't have helped," I say. I had given up on my studies within the first semester, unable to keep up. I had written a letter announcing I was staying even before my student visa expired. The letter had, of course, been intercepted.

I hear monkeys lip-smacking somewhere behind us.

"You might be right," he says.

A headache is starting behind my eyes. I would like for him to leave.

"Yours was a situation beyond me," I say.

He nods as if I am wise. "By then, yes, you might be right."

The repetition fills me with rage. I stand and tell him I need to get back to the animals.

He too stands. He offers some pamphlets. *Three Reasons for Single Women to Vote Democrat. Useful Phone*

Numbers. What Does Your Future Look Like? He says I
have to do something. One cannot look at the last four
years and do nothing, he says.

I am a rope bridge over a deep canyon; he is standing
on my cables, rocking and swaying. We will both go over.
I imagine the impact. This is how it will end.

What do I want? To fall alone. I thank him for coming. I tell him good luck with all those voters.

He puts a hand to my face. A monkey's hand, pink
and soft. He was the delicate one, my mother used to say.
She was the hothouse around her husband the orchid,
she used to say.

He tells me he will come again, and it is relief I feel.
What are my desires? How do I know them?

Back in the playroom, I lie on my side, one arm under my
head like a pillow. Two days ago it rained, and the ground
smells less like sand and more like earth. Zeus is using my
body as a shield, peering over my hip at Ripley. He glances
here and there, trying to anticipate her moves. She regards
him and stays to her side of the cage. And then I find tiny
feet and hands moving their way over and around me. He
stands upright on my hip bone. We are both still, waiting
for Ripley to investigate our hair, our skin, our nostrils,
pose her tests. Zeus and I are sharing the same thought:
This could be a good thing, if we survive.

In the morning he's back, this time carrying a cardboard
box. I have been up for hours. Zeus slept as he should

have; I slept almost not at all. But when have I ever slept through the night? Even as an infant, my mother told me, I refused sleep. My father built a makeshift wagon for the back of his bike and rode me around a darkened Beihai Park.

We are on the bench. I have black tea. Zeus negotiates a mango. He has by now begun to take an interest in solid food as something other than a plaything. Sometimes I give him a piece of fruit but cradle him as if it were a bottle.

"Will he bite?" my father asks, and his fear of animals returns to me. It occurs to me that it must have cost him something to come here to this animal place.

I shake my head and offer him tea.

He says he is too full already.

I offer again.

No, no, he shakes his head.

The third time, he accepts. In my country, this is the way.

It is as if a quarter century has not passed between us. I have spoken more Chinese in the last day than in the last twenty-five years, though we have said nothing of substance. You would think that a forty-nine-year-old so long in this country would be more like a middle-aged American. But the Chinese woman was there all the time.

He holds out the box. "Some photographs I managed to save." He coughs into his shoulder. "The family, the house. Your mother."

Zeus picks at the cardboard, then pulls his fingers back to smell them.

"I thought you might want them," he says, and there, this life disappears, a small, fragile thing next to that other place, my first life.

He's gone again, and Zeus and I sit on my scratchy brown couch and examine the photographs. We're missing another session with Ripley. I told Greta, the Swede, that Zeus seemed a little worn out.

I have pulled my curtains and left the lights off. Perhaps we will look as if we are resting.

The photos are the ones that hung on my parents' bedroom wall. Their wedding portrait. The extended family on the occasion of my birth. Aunts, uncles, and cousins, my father, my mother, and me, the sober infant bundled in padded cotton clothing. It has been so long since I've been the center of anything that the image startles me. "Here," I say to Zeus, who is picking at the zipper of my sweatshirt. "This is me." His gaze follows my finger to the glass and then he is back to the zipper.

How did my father save these when everything was confiscated or destroyed or both? What else could've happened to the household of a former Red Guard who had fled to the United States? Even in this country, I heard the stories. And still I did nothing.

Sally knocks and walks in. She takes in the scene. "I hear he's not quite up to snuff today," she says. She sits beside us on the couch and rubs his ear with a finger and thumb. He closes his eyes and leans into her hand. He knows how to receive care, if not yet how to give it.

"Seems okay to me," Sally says. She glances at the photos in my lap. "Better get him out there with Ripley," she adds, rising.

"He's my father," I say.

She bends and examines the family photo. "Big family," she says. "That you in the middle?"

I nod.

Zeus seems to want to leave with her.

"Fat baby," she says.

"Supposed to be a sign of family prosperity," I say.

"What are you doing?" she asks.

Zeus makes his way to the kitchen, opens the fridge, and gets a hard-boiled egg from the bowl on the bottom shelf. He brings it to me to crack. It's cold.

"I left him there," I say. "Things happened to him, and I stayed here." The only way I can say these things is to avoid looking at her. I realize some part of me has been waiting all these years for her to decide I'm not worth the trouble. When people disappoint her, her face registers genuine pain.

Zeus tugs at my wrist. He wants me to peel the egg for him.

Sally sets her hands on her hips, in the manner of a pregnant woman.

"What happened to him?" she asks.

I tell her he was arrested. I don't even know for how long.

"Maybe you should ask," she says.

She is wearing soft-soled sandals with socks. She likes padding beneath her feet. She says she likes to think she's feeling the earth the way the baboons do.

"Maybe you should ask," she repeats.

"I'm ashamed," I tell her.

"What could you have done?" she asks.

"I don't know," I say. I crack the shell against my knee and hand the egg to Zeus, who sets to work peeling.

"Maybe nothing," she says. She sounds impatient. "Maybe everything. Maybe something in between. Whatever it was, he's here. Your father is here. What does he want?"

I don't know, I tell her. Zeus is filling my cupped hand with pieces of shell. He is a tidy monkey.

Sally moves to the door, shaking her head. "Perhaps to forgive you," she says.

I don't deserve it, I tell her. Her briskness with me is like sour milk settling in my stomach. I want to be admired by this woman.

She opens the door and midday sun slants across the room. "That's something we don't get to decide," she says.

She points at Zeus. "Bring him out to Ripley," she says. She leaves the door open behind her.

Two days go by and he doesn't come. The news is filled with talk of paper trails and voter intimidation. "He's busy," Sally suggests when she sees me checking the driveway yet again. She still sounds impatient. "All those volunteers should get medals," she adds.

The third morning, Greta and I are sitting against the fence beside each other, our legs outstretched, our monkeys on our laps. They play with our clipboards. We monitor the alliance. Sometimes they reach across to touch each other. Yesterday, Zeus offered his missing hand and Ripley ignored it. Today she sniffs at it. So, progress. Once we introduce them to the kindergarten troop it will be all action and speed. Baboons play rough. They have a high tolerance for pain. A troop is nothing but a continual establishment of dominance. There the young ones will need to remember the intimacy and quiet of the playroom. And we mothers will need to remind ourselves that the roughness is a good and natural thing.

My father returns and introduces himself, in perfect English, to Greta.

"Chou," Greta says. "Like Yuan."

He sees my face and says, "It is a common name."

She shrugs, discreet, and takes Ripley off to the supply room.

My father asks for a walk. I tell him he can help me take the garbage bins to the end of the drive. He seems pleased with the responsibility. I fit Zeus into his sling, and Father and I each grab two of the large wheeled bins and maneuver them down the road. There was wind last night, and we push palm fronds out of our way with our feet.

We carted coal bricks for the house's stoves from the neighborhood shed this way, each of us taking a handle of our crooked wheelbarrow. I wonder if he remembers. I wonder if he remembers it as burden or blessing. It seems to me that all memories demand such a decision.

As we pull the bins, he tells me about his life. Not how he got there, but where he has arrived. New York City. A job teaching science to brilliant city children at a highly competitive public school. A modest home on Staten Island. On one side of him, a Korean family. On the other, Russians. Third Aunt and Uncle are in Arizona. Two of their children in Canada. The others in China. He went to visit last year.

What had I imagined? That they'd all been executed?

At the end of the drive, we line up the bins and wipe our brows. Zeus is asleep against my side. Father pulls a small plastic sleeve from his pocket. More photos: My father with a Chinese woman with short hair and silver earrings. A middle-aged man with his arms around a white woman and a vaguely Asian-looking pair of girls. My father leans over my shoulder and points. Here is his wife. Here is her son and his family. Two doctors; twin girls. They live in Manhattan, nearby.

He smells as he always has. His pipe and the chemicals from his lab, like a gas leak through wet leaves. He can't have been in his lab for decades. I can't think how to keep standing, but I do.

He wants me to come to New York with him. Here are the photos of what I could be a part of. He says there is a place in this life for me.

After Zeus's introduction to Ripley, they will be introduced to another pair, then the four of them to a third pair. And so on until there are twelve of them, negotiating what it means to be a new troop. After four years, when they are old enough to protect themselves, it might be possible to release them. That is our goal.

"I have to stay," I say.

He looks around. The drive ends at a busy commercial road. Trucks rattle by. "Why?" he asks.

"Why do you want me to come?" I ask.

"Daughter," he says. It is answer and address.

"I didn't help *you*," I say.

"I'm not offering help to you," he says. "I'm asking it of you."

"I didn't help you," I say again, different emphasis on different words.

He is quiet and puts a finger to Zeus's head. "It's easier to touch him when he's sleeping," he says.

I am not afraid of animals, but I have often felt the same way.

"I didn't ask you for help," he says.

"What happened to you?" I ask. "When I didn't come home, what happened?"

"Only things that happened to many," he says.

"You were arrested," I press.

"An ordinary occurrence," he says.

Zeus has woken up, bothered and cranky. I offer him my finger to suck on.

"I don't deserve your forgiveness," I say.

His eyes fill with a sadness I have not seen before. "It's one thing," he says, "to have chosen this place." He touches my head the way he touched Zeus's. "It's another to choose it again."

After he's gone, instead of taking Zeus back to Ripley and the playroom, I go to the kindergarten. Marta is the volunteer supervising the young troop. She lifts her face to me, curious.

"I'm going to introduce him for a short while," I say.

She glances at Zeus in his sling. "Isn't it a little early?" she asks.

It *is* early, though not by much; two weeks, maybe less. Nevertheless, Sally would not approve.

"We thought we'd give it a try," I say. "The risk is small." I am her senior. I live here, next to Sally. She won't argue.

I sit cross-legged in the middle of the cage. I release Zeus from his sling. He perches on the back of my neck for a moment, then climbs down, turning and turning in my lap.

The others swing and fly at us with a swiftness filled with power and grace. One of them knocks my shoulder backward. Another climbs across my head and shoulders and tries to groom my eyes. There is constant movement. Feet and hands collide. Zeus tries to squeeze under my thigh. His ears flatten; he churrs and chirps, keeping his gaze from the others. I, too, avert my eyes, submitting to the aggression of the group.

"Yuan," Marta says, alarmed.

I close my eyes. The baboons pull at my hair, tooth-grind at Zeus. He emerges to make the fear grimace and the sharp yak of an alarm call.

Marta leaves the cage quickly.

Why *did* I choose this place? What were we Red Guards but a pack of monkeys? I am embarrassed by the simplicity of the analogy.

I lie back. Zeus burrows into my neck. The others are calming. I miss already the power and zeal of their investigations.

Sally takes my lunch period to talk with me. We sit on her porch. She understands it's a difficult time. I must tell her if I need a break, time to work things out. It wouldn't be ideal; it will be more problematic for Zeus if the bond with me is broken at this point. He's on the verge of beginning to express caretaking behavior. It's our job to do all we can to encourage that. "It's not that this was such an enormous setback," she says, "but we're in the business of training ourselves out of a job." If I'm not in a position to do that, I must let her know.

Shame fills my throat like pond water. I am prevented from speech.

She leans over, her face inches from mine. "I won't think less of you," she says. "You should know that by now."

And, again, I am crying.

She stands, regards me patiently for a moment, and then heads back to her monkeys.

I cry off and on for the rest of the day. In the middle of the sleepless night, I take Zeus and the pickup, drive fifty miles north, and check into a motel. I curl up on top of the covers and make distressed noises. Zeus is worried. Other than that, he seems much the same. He crawls across my face, tries to sit on my chest. I stay curled and he settles for under my arm.

I imagine Sally discovering my absence. These are adolescent thoughts, I know.

By day two, he's keeping his distance. Once or twice, he looks behind the curtains. His diaper is cumbersome. He helps himself to water from the bathroom faucet. Sally claims every mistake we trainers make sets the animals back months, maybe years. But Sally is not a scientist.

I haven't moved from the bed. I see what I can from where I am. I could stay here. Why not? I understand it as a fantasy.

Anger, guilt, and sadness roll through me like the waving of a flag. How to differentiate between the three? Even if I couldn't have helped my father, what about the others? Friends, neighbors, teachers, strangers whose names we revolutionaries threw around a room like a child's game?

Zeus turns on the TV. There is the president, his troop behind him. Americans think it is only halfway around the world where poor decisions are made, where lies are spoken as truth. *This* is why I chose this place: here a troop of monkeys is a troop of monkeys. It was not to get away from where I had been. It was to find it again.

Before light on day three, Zeus makes his way onto the bed. He sits behind my head and makes the two-syllable call of moderate distress. He picks at my hair, combing through it with his stubby fingers. He sits on his haunches and pretends to eat the things that he has found. Caretaking. He is imitating the way I have done it for him. My exaggerated concentration is mirrored in his pink, wrinkled brow.

We never know if they're learning from what they see. And then we do, the behavior as natural as genetics, a reintroduction to the self. And we are glad, for them and for us.

I should congratulate him. He especially likes applause.

He wraps and unwraps my hand, exposing and containing the emptiness he finds there.

"Okay," I say to myself as if I mean it, sitting up.

Zeus and I will continue our work. And after him, there will be more monkeys and more work. My father will write letters. And I will write back. There will be success and failure. None of us get to determine how much of either.

Gently, I rub the pucker of Zeus's missing hand and pull him onto my shoulder.

"Okay," I say to him. "Time to go home."

KISS ME SOMEONE

HOWEVER MANY YEARS AGO, NATALIE AND HER HUSBAND used to amuse each other with the deal-breaker conversation. Over dinner or drinks, they would list the deal-breakers of a first date—NRA membership, pro-life bumper stickers, gold chains, cologne—then move on to what would blow up a thirty-year life together: abuse, adultery, other kinds of extremity. The secular Jewish investment banker with a wife and three kids who announces he's going to become a rabbi: *that* woman got to jump ship.

Now Natalie thinks of the things that deserved to be deal breakers but that you let slip while you waited for further evidence or extenuating circumstances. And that now, almost four decades down the road, are off-limits, unfair game, since you took them off the table yourself. They sequestered themselves in their own little room, emerging for purposes of mockery and torment.

She makes herself unexpectedly grim thinking about this in the car on the way home from dinner at the new Brazilian place. She's driving. Her husband of thirty-five years rides beside her studying the darkened margins of the road with a toad's interest. When she's at her grimmest, she thinks of him that way. When she's not, she looks at him and remembers what she fell in love with.

The restaurant was good, but not good enough to justify the half-hour drive. Why is it always a moonless night where they live? What was the point of having moved to the country? She misses the city's illumination, the way night held the comfort of the fabricated.

She slows, not wanting to arrive before her twins are asleep.

Her husband, his name is Lloyd, reaches into a jacket pocket and pulls out a container of floss. He reels off a long strand with the grace of a fly-fisherman and winds it around his index fingers.

He flosses. Bits of food escape his teeth. One hits the windshield like an insect on the wrong side of the glass.

"What are you doing?" she asks.

"What does it look like I'm doing?" he answers, equaling her tone.

"Don't," she says.

He pauses, the floss between molars. "Why not?" he says, genuinely baffled.

She can't look at him. She drives. She concentrates on the chill of the steering wheel beneath her ungloved hands. What's she doing here? The edges of the woods fly past in the headlights. She wishes for something to make her slam on the brakes and spin out.

"Isn't it pretty to think so?" she quotes aloud.

Her husband saws the floss between another two molars. "I never know what you're talking about," he says.

"Stop it," she says.

"Stop what?" he says.

She's suddenly inescapably sad. The sad of keening dolphins. She feels as though she might pass out.

"Have you ever thought about becoming a rabbi?" she asks.

"No," he says.

It's one thing she likes about him after all these years—his willingness to take everything she says seriously.

"What about violence?" she asks. "Have you ever wanted to hit me?"

He stops flossing. "You mean, like a role-playing kind of thing?"

He seems intrigued and her sadness plunges to new depths.

"No," she says.

And now they're home and the girls are asleep and he's following her around like a puppy who has spied the biscuit box atop the fridge. He keeps trying to direct her attention to the stairs, at the top of which they'll find the bedroom, with its four-poster bed and her drawerful of stockings, which, he'll never admit to her, he has on occasion when alone wrapped around his wrist and neck, breathing slowly while he pulls with the deftness of a former yachtsman, which he is.

She checks the girls' schedules for the next day. She programs the coffeemaker for the morning. She fills the dishwasher with the dishes the twins always ignore. She closes the garage door and circles the house like a butler shutting lights. It seems to him that her list of things to do is never-ending. It seems to him he's never on that list.

When she pulls out the two-day-old Sunday paper and settles on the couch in the TV room, he stands behind her for a moment, trying to guess which article she's reading. His lab partner in college once told him, both of them bent over a computer screen, that he had a good scanning eye. "Are you flirting?" he'd asked. "No," she said. He should've known. No one ever flirts with Chinese men.

Natalie turns the page and absorbs herself in the weddings. He touches the back of her head. Her hair is the color of lava. Her scalp is warm. It used to be that she could make him come by kissing his wedding ring.

"I'm going to bed," he says.

She moves her head almost imperceptibly, and he drops his hand.

Her husband is a banker. He's paid for this house and the girls' tuition and the shoes on her feet and the couch under her ass. She pays for nothing. It bothers her more than it should, and him less, but he's a kind, safe man, and 2008 has been a complicated year to be a banker. She knows all this. "All I want to do is read this paper," she finally says. "I never get to read the paper anymore."

"Okay," he says. "You read."

Upstairs, he drops his toothbrush on the floor. He picks it up and snaps it in two. Then he breaks hers. He pads down the hall to the twins' bathroom and breaks theirs. He carries all the pieces back to his bathroom and tucks them into his wife's toiletry kit. Later, when she comes to bed, she'll want to apologize, to talk about why she says and does the things she says and does, and he'll pretend to be asleep. Later still, when she discovers the broken toothbrushes, he'll shrug, and she'll let it slide.

It's a Wednesday and that means lunch with Susan, whom, since her divorce, the other wives call Poor Susan. To her face. Natalie is in the bathroom of the worse of the two Chinese restaurants in town looking at her best friend's new breasts. The two of them are squeezed into a stall and trying to keep their voices down. *Kiss Me Someone* is scratched into the metal door behind Susan. Her shirt is up and Natalie is trying to keep space between her own body and the new breasts.

"What do you think?" Susan says, gleeful. She told Natalie over dumplings that the new boyfriend loves them and that he says they turned out even better than he'd hoped. Apparently Susan now spends a lot of time running around the house with her shirt off laughing until the guy catches her.

It's been decades since Natalie has used the words *boyfriend* or *fake boobs* in a sentence about anyone she knows. She wonders if this is what her fifties will be like. She's speechless. The breasts seem engorged, like those of a nursing mother. They look heavy. "How much do they weigh?" she finally asks.

Susan smiles as if this were just the right question. "A pound," she says.

"A *pound*?"

Susan nods.

"Together?" Natalie asks.

"Each," Susan says.

"*Each*?" Natalie repeats.

Susan nods. "Do you want to touch them?"

Natalie's unsure of the etiquette here. Her friend arches her back, and Natalie reaches out a hand. They feel as swollen as they look. She tries to touch them in a way that won't give either of them too much pleasure. They have the vaguely repulsive velvety feel of a newborn animal.

"Very nice," she says, withdrawing her hand and tucking it into her jacket pocket.

At home that night she tells the girls about it. They're sixteen, and at least as a parent, Natalie believes in full disclosure. Anna wrinkles her nose but barely looks up from her math. She pronounced Susan a lost cause a long time ago. Emily takes the story more seriously. Emily takes everything more seriously. "Do they make her happy?" she asks. "If they make her happy, I don't see the problem. She's not *hurting* anyone."

Anna snorts.

Lloyd comes into the kitchen and feels the conversation close. "Who's not hurting anyone?" he asks.

The girls return to their homework. Natalie turns back to the sink, thinking about Emily's question.

"Hi, Daddy," Anna finally says, with real care. "No one. Girl talk."

That night, he can't sleep. He stands at the kitchen sink drinking a glass of milk. He's wearing plaid jammy pants and a white undershirt and when he sees his reflection in the window, he looks just like himself.

When he climbs back into bed, Natalie wakes.

"Can't sleep?" she asks, her voice low. Her eyes closed, she reaches over and strokes his forehead and tells him what she and the girls were talking about. He understands her inclusion as pity but is grateful nonetheless.

He doesn't care about Susan and her breasts.

"I miss you," he says, watching her. A strand of her lava hair hangs against her pale cheek. Beneath her lids, her eyes are the palest blue. He thinks one day she might combust, leaving behind nothing but ash.

"Here I am," she says, her eyes still closed.

"I know," he says, but he doesn't. When they met, he was eighteen, she was twenty-four. They worked for the same catering company one summer. Word was she'd been on her own since she was sixteen, when her mother took off the final time. Her father had never been around long enough to leave. Even in black and white, she stood out. Their boss had gotten Lloyd's name wrong the whole summer. Late one night, his mom forgot to pick him up, and Natalie offered him a ride. The other waiters hooted when he got into the car. She reached across him to give them the finger.

"Don't worry about them," he said, noting that his feet were on what seemed to be a pile of her fine washables.

She laughed. "This is just a ride," she said. "To your mother's house."

Everyone had wanted her, and she'd chosen him. Even after all these years, he spends his days waiting for her to come to her senses.

She opens her eyes and climbs on top of him. She tells him to close his eyes. She tells him he's her guy. He doesn't know which is more intoxicating, the reassurances from her body or her words. When he starts to come, she tells him to keep his eyes closed.

Afterward, she rests on top of him, her face in his pillow. "What are you thinking?" he finally says.

"Nothing," she says. "Just resting."

In the morning, the twins are a united front. "Don't ever do that to us again," Emily says to her parents.

"Really," Anna says. "Get a hotel room."

"Years from now, we'll be spending months on this in therapy."

Natalie is somewhere between pleased and ashamed.

Lloyd tries to recall how loud he was. A couple of years ago, he told her that he wished she would come on to him more often.

"You wish I'd *what*?" was all she ever said on the subject.

"And another thing," Emily says. "Where are our toothbrushes?"

Winter comes and goes. April arrives in a tantrum of mud and rain. The lawn is like a pockmarked child. The forsythia refuses to bloom. The rhododendrons are dying. When she asks the lawn guy if the willow will ever stop shedding, he explains that it's a dirty tree.

And then during a heat wave in May, one of the girls' classmates jumps from the roof of the school into a sea of recessing fourth graders, and Natalie and Lloyd run into one of her exes at the Starbucks. Of all her exes, and the number is legion, this one was the most extreme in all regards. Best lover, least good-looking, most likely to be living in his parents' garage for the rest of his life, most likely to go through her purse, most likely to call her on things she deserved to be called on, most violent, least repentant. Even twentysomething Natalie, the Natalie who wanted nothing more than to wrap herself in the extremity of others, understood that as far as Cullen was concerned, *there be monsters*. When she tried to break up with him the first time, he slid his hand down the front of her jeans and put his finger inside her, pulling her onto her tiptoes to meet his waiting mouth. When he was done, he slid his finger away and said, "So?"

The sight of him in his black jeans—she swears they're the *same* jeans—and his black Cons is so convincing that it's Lloyd who she stares at in vague incomprehension.

"What?" her husband says.

If rage is at her core, her husband is always drilling away at her surface. He's always saying *what*. Figure it out, she wants to yell. The girls had a nursery school teacher who told them over and over to use their words. Use your words, she wants to tell him, but never does.

"It's Cullen," she says.

"Who?" he asks, looking around.

She attempts a low groan, but it comes out sounding like a whimper.

"What?" he says.

Cullen in Black is standing there smiling. He always looks as if he's stoned. It was part of his initial appeal. "Holy crap," he says. "Natalie, Nattie, Nat."

He liked to say her name three times, shorter and shorter. Her therapist at the time said it was his way of disappearing her. The therapist also said it was not a good sign that she found this attractive. Natalie said she was sure he was right.

Later when she's gotten the call from the school and heard from other mothers that one boy had to be taken shopping by his teacher because parts of the girl who had jumped had gotten *on* him, when she's heard that the girl had taken the time and effort to unscrew the safety bars on the windows, and that the mother is a single mother, and the little brother somewhat disturbed, when she's heard more than she thinks she can stomach about a sixteen-year-old girl's sadnesses, she hears that the girl had checked with her younger brother to make sure he'd be safely in gym when she jumped. But instead the brother had been on his way back to the main building, his sister's body in front of the entrance. Inside Natalie, something large gives way: the girl had tried to keep her sadnesses from the person she'd cared about most, and had failed.

After she packs lunches for the girls, empties the dishwasher, and waters the plants, she calls Cullen. He always loved her most after she'd been in tears.

"It's me," she says. "I'd like to see you."

He laughs. "I don't know, Mrs. Natalie. Probably not such a good idea."

She sniffs.

"Have you been crying?" he asks.

His place is not his parents' garage, but it's pretty close. It's on the side of town she doesn't have much call to pass through. The manager's apartment in a thirty-unit complex. There's a name like Oak Village and a pool facing the road. There are carports. Cullen's embarrassed about the whole thing, and she thinks about joking that she hopes she doesn't run into her maid. His expression makes her wonder if she's somehow spoken out loud.

"I'm sorry," she says, as if she has. She sits on a couch that she thinks she may recognize from his parents' garage. "I don't know what's wrong with me," she says, and she's crying again. She wants to explain, but it's not in her to do that, not even to try.

After they have sex, he watches her dress, and he says, "All the right curves in all the right places, babe," and she thinks she may never have been more tired of herself in her life. She starts crying again. He takes it as some kind of homage. He flexes his bicep and then wraps his arm around her. "It's okay," he tells her. "You just cry, cry, cry."

When she calms down, he says, "You always were a crier," and it's true that she hasn't felt this way since she was eighteen, like she needs arm after arm around her to remind herself that nothing helps, that she's a game she's already lost.

"Jesus Christ," she says aloud. "I'm ridiculous."

"What?" he says, and she starts to laugh.

"You sound like my husband," she says, and she laughs harder.

He watches her. "Hey," he says. "Not that I'm making any judgment calls here, but you seem pretty fucked up. You might want to get some help with that, you know?"

"Great," she says. "I've got Cullen fucking Marks telling me I'm fucked up." The mix of rage and sadness makes her feel like she used to during her best highs, right before the nausea.

What did the girl feel like after unscrewing the last bolt from the window bars and setting the screwdriver next to her book bag? Did she have second thoughts? Did she worry about her mother? Her brother? Thank God, she must've been thinking. Thank God.

She's looking at Cullen with such repulsion that even he gets it. "Hey," he says finally. "You called me."

"You're right," she says. "You always were." She looks at him. "Come back to the house for dinner," she says.

Despite himself, a small smile plays across his mouth.

She leans over him, her hair curtaining their faces. She runs the tip of her tongue under his top lip.

A sound escapes him. "You're bad," he says, snaking his hand up the inside of her leg.

She thinks of Cullen in her house. It's a terrible, terrible idea. "So?" she says.

At home, they stand in her front hall. It's darker inside than it is out, and she remembers with some disappointment that Lloyd is picking Anna up from practice. She glances at her watch. Sometimes they stop for donuts. She hears the small sounds of crying somewhere. She listens more carefully. It's Emily. Emily always cries as if mildly embarrassed about the whole thing, staying sad and ashamed for days afterward. Anna's the tropical storm of sadness. She sobs and sobs and then whatever mattered suddenly no longer does.

Natalie would like to leave. Get back in the car, put it in neutral, and roll as quietly as possible down the driveway and onto the road. She closes her eyes. "Let's go," she says to Cullen. "This was a bad idea."

"Someone's crying," he says.

She can smell him on her skin. When they were going out, he liked to make her come with his hand, and then hold his wet fingers to her mouth. She never liked the taste of herself. She distracted him from doing that whenever she could.

Emily's cries aren't any louder, but they aren't stopping either.

"Stay here," she says, and heads down the hall to Emily's room. It's empty. Emily is in Natalie's room, sitting cross-legged on her bed like a tableau of Young Natalie. She looks up at her mother.

"Where have you been?" she says.

Natalie doesn't answer. She's never seen her daughter sadder.

"I'm sad," Emily says. She's trying to stop crying, but she can't. Her hands wipe at her face.

"That makes two of us," Natalie says.

Emily cries harder.

Everything Natalie thinks of saying is complicated. There are things we can never know about each other and ourselves. Maybe even for sixteen-year-olds who are lucky in so many ways, there are things that'll never be right. But all of her wisdom seems pathetic. So she sits on the bed and watches her daughter cry. Hair is stuck to her face. Her hands are wet with wiped tears. She looks at her mother. "*Do* something," she says.

Natalie thinks of Cullen waiting in the foyer. Maybe he's moved to the kitchen, checked the fridge for something to eat. Maybe he's perusing the framed photos on the living room sideboard. Maybe Lloyd and Anna have come home. She feels like the shell of something. A spider's victim, or an Egyptian corpse. Her daughter looks as if she's treading water in the ocean.

"What's wrong with you?" Emily says. She's stopped crying.

Natalie tells her she doesn't know and tries to smile. Emily stares at her. "I'm a mystery to myself," Natalie adds.

"You're my mother," Emily points out.

"People get sad," Natalie says. "People do sad things when they're sad."

"Stop," Emily tells her. She takes a huge breath. "Just shut up."

Natalie would like to tell her that although these feelings will never go away, she'll learn how to navigate their waters. That happiness is something we all deserve.

"I don't want to lie to you," she says instead.

"You're not sad," Emily says. "You're mean."

Heat spreads across Natalie's chest. "I'm both," she says.

"*Why?*" Emily says.

Natalie strokes her forearm.

"Mommies know all," Emily says. It's something Natalie used to tell them when they were trying to figure out how she knew they were lying about something.

And then Cullen is in the doorway. He leans against the frame as if waiting for a friend. "Everything okay in here?" he asks.

The sight of him on the threshold of her bedroom uncoils something slippery in Natalie's chest. Emily looks at her and then at him. "Who are you?" she asks.

He nods in Natalie's direction. "Old friend of your mother's," he says.

"Really," Emily says blandly.

Her face is puffy and wet, and Natalie says to Cullen, "She doesn't like other people to see her crying."

"Mom," Emily says sharply.

"She also doesn't like other people to know private stuff about her," Natalie says.

"Mom," Emily repeats.

Cullen says, "Wonder where she gets that," and crosses to the chair next to the bed. It's where Natalie throws her clothes. He's sitting on her nightgown.

"What kind of old friend?" Emily says. It's not clear which of them she's asking.

He stretches his legs out and looks up at Natalie. "You want to handle that one, Mom?" he says.

She can't feel the muscles in her face. She looks at him with an expression she hopes contains sufficient warning.

He smiles and leans forward. "We were crazy in love," he tells Emily. "Like you can't believe. Out of this world."

Nothing about him suggests he's teasing. Emily is staring at him.

He heads to the bed and sits between them. "It's the truth," he says. "Ask your mom."

Natalie stands. "We should go," she tells him.

Every part of Emily suggests high alert. "What's he doing here now?" she asks her mother.

Cullen suddenly looks worn-out and angry. "Yeah," he says. "What's he doing here now?"

Natalie shakes her head. She says now that he just should leave.

His laugh is a short bark.

Emily is more alarmed. "Mom?" she says.

Anna and Lloyd appear in the doorway. They take in the scene.

"Who are you?" Anna says to Cullen.

She exchanges a look with her sister.

"Natalie?" Lloyd says.

Her husband of thirty-five years, and the father of her children: there he is, regarding her as if she's the only person in the room.

Lloyd keeps his eyes on his wife and makes his way to the bed. She looks as though she's forgotten who he is, but he tells himself that he can make himself come into clear focus for her. He sits behind her and puts his arm around her. If the bed is the ocean he tries to be a tiny boat.

Cullen is still on the bed beside them. "Hey, Lloyd," he says.

Lloyd holds her tighter. The guy is a child. The thought of him with Natalie should make him laugh, but it doesn't.

Emily tells Cullen warily, "I think you should go."

Cullen smiles at her and flicks the edges of her hair against her cheek. Then he turns his attention to Lloyd.

"Please," Natalie says. Lloyd can't tell which of them she's addressing, but he turns to Cullen and says, "I'm going to have to ask you to leave."

Cullen smoothes the bedspread between them and shakes his head. "Sorry, comrade. No can do. She invited me," he says. "Isn't that right, Mrs. Natalie?"

"Quit fucking around," she says. She turns to Lloyd. "I can explain."

Lloyd releases her. "Just be quiet," he says.

"Honey," he says to Emily, his voice steady. "Go with your sister and wait in the other room."

Nobody moves.

"What's wrong with me?" Natalie says, and Lloyd has never been angrier with her, but he says, "Nothing. Nothing's wrong with you." Because if he says it, maybe it'll be true.

But she knows it's not the ocean rocking their boat; it's her. Just to see what happens. She could tell them all this. She could say, *I do such damage.* She could say, *I jump and the boat bucks and sways.*

Cullen says, "You know what I think about all the time? You remember the story you told me about that camp you went to?"

Everyone looks at him.

"That day you did those things with the horse? I can't remember what it was called."

Natalie's trying to focus on him.

"Remember?" he says with some impatience.

She shakes her head. She doesn't.

He says, "When I think about you, I think about your face telling me that story."

Lloyd has reddened slightly and says with a control that lets Natalie know just how angry he is, "You need to leave."

Cullen nods as if Lloyd has said something very wise. "You need to ask your wife what I'm doing here," he says.

And then she does remember: flying lead changes, changing leads at the canter in the air between two strides, designed to make changes in direction easier and more balanced. The day she couldn't get them, her instructor let all the other students go, and slowed Natalie and her horse to a walk, going over what she'd been going over for hours: A good lead change would appear effortless in both the horse's actions and the rider's cues. She had to be able to feel where the horse's feet were in the canter sequence. She had to allow the change to happen beneath her. "You *know* all this," her instructor said. "So show me." And she sent Natalie back and forth, cantering on the long diagonals across the arena, oily dirt flying up around her horse's hoofs, the sun long gone behind the barn. "Swap your leg position," her instructor called out. "Balance into the hand. Throw your weight. Show me. Now." And Natalie couldn't, and couldn't, and then she could, and the feeling was otherworldly, the ripple and shift of the horse's giant muscles a liquid landslide beneath her. She'd formed a partnership with the horse, but even more than that, she hadn't: the animal was like a willed extension of *her* power. Together they'd shown off a little. Her usually gruff instructor had been genuinely thrilled. "Now you're going places," she'd said.

"Flying lead changes," Natalie tells the group. She composes her face.

"Natalie," Lloyd says. His voice is full of warning and humiliation and betrayal. She's never told him that story.

"I'm sorry," she says to both men, her voice calm. "I need a couple of minutes."

Both men stand, but don't move.

She hasn't been on a horse in years. She says, "The best thing about flying changes is the moment when all four of the horse's legs are off the ground. The suspension phase, it's called." She beckons to Anna, who comes over and joins her sister on the bed. "Please," she says again to both of the men. "Just a few minutes."

Lloyd lets Cullen out of the room first, then turns back to his daughters. "I'll be right down the hall," he says. "You call me if you need me."

The girls nod and move closer to each other on the bed. Natalie listens to the sounds of the men moving away from the bedroom, then she turns to her girls and takes them in. They eye her warily.

"Hey," she says.

"Hey," they say together.

She wants to be back at the beginning of something. She wants the possibility of that best self to be waiting for her at the end of the long unhappy lesson. So she'll show them what she's known all along. She'll explain what Cullen's doing there. She'll explain why she called him and what she needed. She won't leave anything out. *Full disclosure*, she thinks, wiping her face. She can teach them. How to throw their weight, change their lead. Come on, she'll say to her girls. Let's show off a little.

MAGIC WITH ANIMALS

KAYLA DID WHAT SHE ALWAYS DID WHEN HER LIFE BROKE apart in its usual ways: she called Sable, the closest thing to a mother she'd had. Sable had never outright refused her anything, even if she had offered a *Really?* and *Are you sure?* every so often. The woman was a saint. She walked into a room and made everyone in it better people.

It was only when Henry answered that Kayla remembered that Sable was sick, and that whatever Kayla needed this time around, she wasn't going to get. But what were her other options? So she stayed on the phone like a stubborn dog with its nose to the door.

She was going on three years in North Carolina with Shaw, and although she wasn't exactly happy, she wouldn't have said she was more miserable than usual. Mr. Magic, Henry called him, because he was an animal trainer and magician. Sable had been, as always, more supportive. But a month ago, Kayla had lost her job; the Food Depot had let a quarter of them go. That meant no rent money, and that meant eviction warnings. Her daughter's public school had started suggesting that Clare's particular needs might be better met elsewhere. And then an ex-girlfriend of Shaw's who turned out to be not so much *ex* as *here and now* showed up at their door again, this time waving a pregnancy test.

And now Shaw was telling Kayla that if they just gave the woman the money to take care of the pregnancy and then some, she'd go away for good. He could guarantee it. Kayla reminded him that when it came to his finances "and then some" wasn't really in his bag of tricks. His face reminded her how much they could still hurt each other. Maybe that meant they were still in love.

She'd fallen for the way he had with animals, not just dogs and cats, but the exotic and dangerous— howler monkeys and tigers, baboons and even a taipan. He expressed the same care for spiders as for Lab puppies, an egalitarianism that had particular appeal for her. His show was called *Animal Magic* with the tag line *The Art of Dreaming*. When she'd asked for the secrets to his tricks, he told her the only trick was figuring out what they would do anyway and then building the illusion around that. Then he'd kissed her, demonstrating that the animals were just doing what was natural to them.

But even with the ex-girlfriend still waiting on their front porch, Kayla told him that she was just worn out.

Did he want to know what she wanted? Always, he answered in his glass-half-full way. She said she wanted rest. She hadn't felt rested in God knew how long. Maybe ever. Maybe they were like dogs playing rough for too long, and everyone needed to head to their opposite corners for a while. Could they do that?

He'd knelt on the floor and leaned against her. She felt his belt buckle against her thigh. That's not what you want, he said with such confidence that she thought he might be right. He'd told her once that it wasn't the animals' job to understand; it was his job to explain.

Later he suggested that Henry and Sable could help. They'd *want* to help, and, he added, she wasn't going to find what they had going for them anywhere else. He made a back-and-forth gesture between her chest and his. I'm on your side, he said, and waited.

It was what he said to reluctant animals. She hadn't answered. Later, she thought, *I don't even know what game we're playing, let alone which side I'm on.*

So she'd taken off without telling him, leaving him to deal with the eviction notice and the pregnant girlfriend. She packed the car with what she could and stored the rest in a friend's basement. She picked Clare up from school and called Henry from the road an hour into the drive.

Henry was still getting used to being the one who answered the phone. Sable had always fielded their calls. He had liked it that way.

He didn't want Kayla to come but she didn't seem concerned about that, and he hadn't known how to insist without being mean. She wasn't their daughter but as far as Sable had been concerned, she might as well have been. She'd lived next door as a kid and had spent more time at their place than her own. Her house had featured powdered Crystal Light in the cupboards, rented furniture, and an unhappy mother overmatched by the world. The curtains were perpetually drawn, but one day the girl squeezed her way around their fence, wondering if maybe they'd like to see how she could hula-hoop and walk at the same time.

She'd liked their house, and he had always been an easy mark for anyone who liked his house. He and Sable had designed it—bookshelves and windows their guiding principles—and his father had helped him build it, the one nice thing his father had done for him, Sable had pointed out. When he'd argued that she was being too harsh, she looked at him and said, "Henry. The man left you his straw hat. In his will."

Before then Kayla had never seen a ceiling made of wood or eaten a bagel or heard music with no words. But mostly, it appeared, she had never known someone like Sable. She shadowed her. She seemed disconcerted by Sable's impromptu hugs. Sable made cheesecake and whole fish cooked in sea salt. She recited poems to the girl and sang her songs from her childhood. They took turns drawing intersecting parts of mythological creatures.

Henry engineered bridges and had shown Kayla the plans for the drawbridge over the bay. And though her eyes sometimes glazed over politely, she asked him to read words like *trunnion* and *cofferdam* rendered in his precise all-caps print. "Bascule bridge," he'd heard her whisper to herself. He'd heard her tell her daughter it was French for *seesaw*. "I know," Clare answered. It was her response to pretty much everything. Everyone had thought it was cute until Clare had the first few full-on panic attacks, and then Kayla started second-guessing everything, at a loss about whether there were patterns to her behavior and if there were, what to do about them.

He hadn't seen Kayla or Clare in three years. Since they'd left with the Snake Charmer. About whom Sable had been more optimistic and Henry hadn't felt in a position to argue. Before he and Sable had married there'd been an abortion that he'd encouraged but had insisted was her decision, and after that, there'd been a life filled with joys and pleasures, but none of them children. Sable had not had to say anything to make him feel responsible. So though Kayla had been trouble a lot of the time, her presence also made him feel relieved and oddly lucky, and he hoped his wife had felt the same.

His wife wasn't doing well. She'd been diagnosed with dementia and her decline had been gradual until it wasn't. He'd told Kayla at the time that he could use some help and some company, but apparently she'd been in the middle of something. Swamped, she'd said. Pulling rabbits out of hats? he'd asked, and then had gotten off the phone angry and envious that she could just get back to her life. Her ties to Sable weren't the kind with clear expectations attached to them. If she came to help, everyone would talk about how she was going above and beyond. If she didn't, no one would blame her. The expectations for him, meanwhile, were like looking into the sun.

And then she called for the first time in months and told him she'd been thinking of driving down. She said a visit was long overdue, as if that had been his fault.

He told her things were going better. The caregiver was working out. She came six days a week. She cooked, she cleaned, she laughed at his jokes. He was teaching her to play chess.

"You taught me to play chess," Kayla said.

"Yes, I did," he said, and went on. Sable liked her, too: Missy. He called her Miss-S-Able. Get it? he asked.

"I get it," Kayla said flatly. Then she told him that she had some time off and that Clare could skip some school.

He reminded her that change bothered Sable and that Kayla must be busy. She answered that they missed him, and that Clare wanted to come. If she didn't know better, she said, she'd think he was trying to keep her away. Just what was he up to down there? she teased. So he retreated to what he always said to her: *Mi casa es su casa.*

After he got off, he predicted to Sable it would take less than a day for the real reason she was coming to emerge. "You watch," he told her, handing her a glass of juice on the porch.

A year earlier she would've sighed and told him it was only money.

He looked at his hands. For Kayla the assumption had always been that they were there to help, as if they were settling some long-standing debt.

Missy came out onto the porch to shake out the bathroom mats.

He watched her and then looked at Sable again. She was still sitting there, silent. "She'll need something," he said to Sable.

Missy took the juice glass from her. "We all need something," she said.

"Do you hear me?" he asked his wife. He missed their conversations. When he was mad, he was mad about that.

Missy laid her hand on his shoulder. "She hears you," she said.

...

They were only two hours into the twelve-hour drive to Miami and already Clare had said "I know" a dozen times. She knew it was a long drive; she knew they would stop soon for lunch. It wasn't sass as much as some kind of resistance. Whenever Clare used the phrase, Kayla felt as if she were watching her daughter set another brick in a wall. A year ago, Clare had freaked out about a home-work project, and then had lost it again on a crowded school bus. She had felt trapped, she told Kayla later.

Like she was going to have a heart attack. Since then, there'd been six similar episodes, but they always passed, and between them she seemed like herself. The counselor the school asked Kayla to take Clare to see had talked about anxious children becoming anxious adults. She described Clare as a sponge soaking up Kayla's fears. She said there were tools to keep those anxieties from getting the better of her, but going to the counselor had *also* made Clare anxious, and when she asked not to go back she looked so agonized that Kayla said okay. She told herself they could always resume the visits later, but then life took over. And maybe this was just who Clare was, anyway.

The cell rang. Clare answered. "Hi Shaw," she said.

Kayla reached her hand out behind her, but Clare scooted to the far side of the back seat, switching the phone to the other ear.

"I know," she said. "Really."

Kayla was pretty sure Shaw liked her daughter more than he'd ever like someone his own age. Maybe Idiot Girl should have the kid after all. She didn't want to think about what it would be like to tell Clare she and Shaw were splitting up. Sable had told her more than once that life was all about expanding your empathetic ground. Kayla had thought it had to do with putting yourself in someone else's shoes and not being overwhelmed by standing there. Sometimes she thought she could do the former. She wasn't all that good at the latter.

Clare looked around. "I don't know," she said. "It's a highway." She said to Kayla, "Where are we?"

Kayla reached her hand back again.

"I don't know, a couple of hours?" Clare said. She scanned the road. "Quinby?" she added.

Kayla flicked her signal and pulled onto the shoulder. Semis passed going eighty. The car shook. She twisted around and held out her hand. "Give me the phone," she said.

Clare looked at her. "Mom wants to talk to you," she said blandly. "Okay," she said. "I will."

Kayla took the phone. "Put your headphones on," she told her.

Clare frowned at her.

Kayla dug in her backpack, coming up with a tangled mess of headphone wires. "Here," she said.

From the cell, Shaw's voice said, "Hello?"

"Put them on," Kayla said.

"Are you talking to me?" Shaw asked.

"They're tangled," Clare said.

"Untangle them," Kayla said.

"Hello?" Shaw said again.

Clare opened her book. "I don't care what you talk about," she said.

Kayla told him she'd call him back and hung up. She tucked the phone into the drink holder and looked at Clare in the rearview.

"We're working out some things," she said.

Clare kept reading.

"I didn't tell him where we were going," Kayla said.

"He said to say hi to Henry and Sable," Clare told her.

Kayla sat there. She had no idea what she was doing. Was she planning on asking Henry for money? Leaving Shaw? If Sable had been Sable, there would've been homemade cheesecake and strong coffee, someone to listen, and gray eyes filled with love. Sable's advice was often hard but almost always right, based as it was in the kind of careful attentiveness Kayla could never achieve. How do you know me so well? she would often ask. I listen, Sable would answer. It's not hard.

Kayla spied on Clare in the rearview. She was concentrating on her book, her lips moving a little as she read. Being a mother before Clare's episodes had seemed intimidating enough. Being a mother now, without Sable, was plain out of Kayla's league.

"Okay, then," Kayla said, flicking her signal and merging back into traffic.

...

They stopped for lunch at a barbecue place called Barbeque! that featured taxidermied squirrels posed in eternal scamper across trees that grew out of the floor. Occasionally a small plastic leaf fell to the table. One landed in Clare's tea. She picked it out while looking at her mother.

Kayla tried to explain about Sable, but every time she started, Clare asked if Sable was going to die.

Kayla didn't know how to answer. Of course she was. Everyone did. But did you die from dementia or its complications, and did the difference even matter? Not right now, she ended up telling Clare. Vague and alarming: her specialty.

She should never have introduced Shaw to them. She had thought that he would find some of the same solace she had, but he'd ended up even more resentful that he had never had anyone like them. And she had had to admit, watching them negotiate their way around conversation with him, that he'd missed out: not only was it easier to absorb solace as a kid, but it was easier to offer it *to* a kid. She'd finished the visit disappointed in all of them, including herself.

Mixing her worlds had never been a good idea. She'd introduced Clare's father to her own mother after they found out about the pregnancy, and her mother spent the whole visit smoking cigarettes with him on the couch, laughing and leaving her hand on his arm for too long. When they left, he'd dismissed Kayla's complaints. She'd hoped Shaw was her chance to break that pattern. She added that to her growing list of mistakes.

Henry and Sable had always helped out when they could, and they'd also always promised there'd be something for her when they were gone. But what did that mean? Sable's recipe box? A Swiss bank account? Kayla didn't know anything about their finances. They seemed fine, but compared to her everyone seemed fine. The only thing of value she'd ever heard them talk about was a painting Sable's father had smuggled out of Europe during the war, and even that seemed more about senti-ment than cash.

At this point, Kayla needed hard promises in tripli-cate. Not just for herself, but for Clare. And she didn't like the sound of Missy. She didn't like to think of some-one else walking around that house opening the draw-ers, touching the sheets.

She supposed the best thing would be to move in. A new school for Clare, and she could play caretaker, she thought gamely. Shaw would work himself out. *Yes*, she thought, feeling decisive. *Okay*.

She held her camera in her lap, thinking they might take a picture. "What's that about?" she asked, pointing to Clare's book. It was called *The Palace of Happiness*. Clare had come home from the library with it.

"It's kind of complicated," Clare said.

Kayla said, "It's got a unicorn on the front. How complicated could it be?"

Clare said, "There's two whole family trees that you have to memorize before you start reading."

Kayla reached for it and Clare cried, "Don't," her voice all panic.

"I just want to *see* it," Kayla said. She shook her daughter's arm, hard. Sometimes that worked.

Clare's tears were starting, but they were the quiet kind, and Kayla counted her blessings.

"It's a library book," she said. "Tons of people have touched it. It's not yours." Why should her girl get *so* upset at these kinds of things? At life? Hadn't Kayla done her best to raise her? Better than *her* mother had ever done? But once she started with questions like that it wasn't too long before she got to the answers. And whatever the answers, there was her daughter, suffering.

They ordered ice cream and she told Clare to finish it and go to the bathroom because once they were on the road she wasn't stopping.

"I know," Clare said.

While they were supposed to be napping Henry brushed Sable's hair with the child-sized brush she liked. Missy had said they should take a siesta before the excitement of the visitors. "I'm not excited," he told her.

"Yes, you are," she said, ushering them into the bedroom.

But they hadn't been able to sleep, so he sat his wife at their bathroom counter and told her he'd do her hair, and talked about Kayla, about the time she'd brought the feral cats home, or the lunatic guy who'd been her prom date, Tiny Tim without the charm. Three-day-old baby Clare in Sable's arms on the porch swing.

She opened her eyes. "We're all so unhappy," she said.

It was the first thing she'd said in days, and as usual he was equal parts gratitude and torment. He smoothed her hair and looked at both of them in the mirror. When had life sped away from them? He should've been more vigilant. He looked at her eyes. They were dimming like the flames of old gaslights. She smelled of shampoo and baby wipes. "Yes, we are," he said.

Minutes away from the house, the car was filled with the particular heat of the setting sun and Clare was asleep. Kayla cracked her window and smoked a cigarette, blowing in the general direction of outside.

Down Palm to Palmetto, and there they were. She pulled into the driveway alongside Henry's car, the sound of the tires on the loose pebbles as familiar as her heartbeat. "Crazy Love" came on the radio. She hadn't heard it in years. She lit another cigarette and listened. Here she was, twenty-eight, a mother, about to step into a house that had always welcomed her, and all she could think was who would love her now that Sable was gone.

She called Shaw back. She asked if he remembered the lemurs. When they were first dating, he'd arranged for her to play with some at a sort of sanctuary. They'd sat on the floor of an enclosure cross-legged, their knees touching. Stay low, the keeper had instructed. The animals took astonishing leaps from floor to jungle gym to rope ladder to the tops of their heads. The lemurs' hands were like leather. Their fur was thick and soft. She'd kept expecting it to hurt when they landed on her, but it never did.

Of course he remembered, he told her.

She was glad. She said he might be right, she might never find what they had anywhere else, but that even she knew they were at the end of their run.

He was quiet for so long she thought he might've put down the phone, but then he said the more he thought about it the more he was sure he couldn't let her go that easy. He didn't sound upset, and something in his voice tipped her from compassion to wariness.

"You're *not* letting me go," she said. "I'm walking away."

It sounded as if he were moving something across the floor. "I don't think so," he said as if he were guessing someone's weight.

She got out of the car and walked into the shade. She'd once seen him separate two fighting dogs by putting his arm between their muzzles. "You've gotta give them something else to fight over," he'd said later.

"Come on," she said. She thought she might cry, she was so tired. "You can't make me love you," she said.

"That's true," he said.

She heard a car start. "What're you doing?" she asked.

"I think you know," he said.

Now she *was* crying. "Come on," she said again. If she got more pathetic and desperate it would only make him more himself, but she didn't seem to have a choice. She wiped her face. "What do you want from me?" she asked.

The engine was running, but she could tell he wasn't driving. She could see him sitting there in their driveway, one wrist on the wheel, the sun on the dust motes in his truck's cab. His sunglasses in his breast pocket or hooked on the visor. His morning coffee mug in the cup holder, a quarter full and cold.

"Okay, then," he said. He didn't say anything else. She listened to him breathe. He'd told her once that breathing was as much a part of magic as hand-eye coordination or small muscle dexterity. He'd held her palm against his chest and breathed, easy and even. "One. Two. Three. Magic," he'd said.

"You think I'm going to just make myself gone until you tell me different?" he said now. He said it like even she must know how unlikely that was.

She didn't answer.

"I don't think so," he said. But she could hear the hurt in his voice.

But then he seemed to switch gears. "If you tell me to go," he said, "that's that."

Her heart clutched the way it did when faced with losing anything. How did regular people tell what was worth keeping and what you were better off without?

He said her name.

"Yes," she said quietly, and she could tell he was offering her a deal.

"Don't ask them for anything," he said.

He outlined his plan. He wanted Sable's painting. He'd be there in two days. He'd call when he was a few hours away. She should leave the door unlocked. That was all she had to do and afterward he'd be gone. Guaranteed. And then he hung up.

She got back in the car, where it was as hot as panting animals. Had he always been that kind of guy, or had she always just believed what she'd wanted about him? She'd known how hurt he'd been that Henry and Sable hadn't embraced him more fully. So maybe her shock was more self-protective than genuine. He'd always said about his animals that if you hurt them they hurt you back.

Clare's hair was sticking to her cheek.

Could they have taken a different turn somewhere? Tried Door Number Three? Maybe people like her always ended up right where she was.

A tall black woman appeared at the car door. "You must be Kayla," she said. "I'm Missy."

Kayla wiped at her eyes and opened the door, and Missy stepped back to let her out. She was probably forty and a head taller, with skin like burnished wood. Her hair was warrior-woman short and her chest flat as a boy's. "Everything okay?" she asked.

Kayla nodded.

"You were out here a long time," Missy said.

Kayla wasn't sure if this required a response.

"She's sleeping," Missy said, bending to look at Clare. "She's beautiful," she added, and for a moment Kayla felt as if she herself were being praised.

They both stood there looking in the car. Missy's gaze slid around. "You brought a lot of stuff."

Kayla had had enough of this conversation. She twisted her hair up and then let it fall. "Well, who knows how long we'll stay," she said lightly.

"Stay as long as you can," Missy said. "They'll be happy to have you."

Henry stood at the sink putting the breakfast dishes in the dishwasher. He was tired. Kayla had offered to clean up, but he'd suggested she help Sable get ready for the day. Things had been tense since her arrival for reasons he didn't have the energy to parse. The attentions his wife now required were relentless even with Missy's help. Was this what fifty years of marriage came down to? He began every day with an engineer's determination to do what was necessary and ended undone and unable to rise from his chair.

If it hadn't been for Missy, he wouldn't have had a dinner to offer them the night before. Three weeks earlier, dinner had meant potato salad in a plastic tub, cold cuts in the store's ziplock bags, milk in its carton. Missy served a hearty chicken casserole, the kind of thing Sable would've made, and homemade corn bread. She spread Sable's slice with a thin layer of honey, tricking her into eating two pieces that way, and then told them she'd see them in the morning. He tried to get her to stay and eat, but she said she had to get home, and when she'd gone, Kayla patted his arm and told him it was good to be here with just family.

He had seen her face as Sable ate, more food on the table than in her mouth, and he wanted to tell her this was nothing. That was another thing about this new life: anger. Had it been there all along? And what was he to do with it?

Clare sat on the high stool by the kitchen counter. He'd never found her easy to talk with. She had always struck him as harboring mild resentments about the world's interruptions. In his opinion, her episodes were those resentments given voice. Just leave her be, he'd advised when Kayla had finally called to tell him what was going on. She'll sort this out on her own. Kayla had reminded him that that was his advice about everything. She hadn't had to say what they were both thinking: If only she could talk to Sable.

But he didn't see what was so wrong with his advice. It seemed the most natural way to see the world: geologically. Plates would shift; mountains would form; lakes would fill to their rims.

"Are you crying?" Clare asked.

These days he was thinking about her even when he wasn't thinking about her. Any kind of rumination took him into waters he didn't know how to navigate. He shook his head.

Clare looked unconvinced.

"So," he began, but then couldn't think of where to go from there.

She looked at him.

"Your clothes are dirty," he said, swiping the sink with the sponge. Where had he gotten his shirt? He tried to remember getting dressed. An image of Missy ironing appeared. She had made him change. They didn't go anywhere but doctors. They didn't have visitors. What difference did their clothes make?

It makes a difference to us, Missy had said. Before he hired her he let Sable stay in her nightdress for days at a time until his guilt got the better of him and he announced a Spa Day: a bath, shampoos and nail trims, Q-tips and lotion.

Now Missy did all the clipping and trimming. But what did that leave him? Something about his wife's unmoored mind had sent her into a kind of no-man's-land of sensory need. Certain smells bothered her. She tested almost everything with her tongue. She wanted treats. He kept the chocolate in a locked cupboard to be doled out as bribery. Sometimes he found her running her fingers against the edges of paper or the air-conditioner vents. She was always reaching into her armpits or under her skirt, and she touched him the same way. In bed she pulled at his penis as if remembering in some inchoate way what they used to do and who they used to be.

She wanted to be touched as well, but he didn't like it. On the rare occasion when he did curl around her in bed, it was like trying to hold a swarm of butterflies.

Touch and talk were both gone. He leaned against the counter, his legs unreliable. "She said she'd stay healthy," he told the sink.

"Are you talking to me?" Clare asked.

He'd forgotten she was there. "Can you keep a secret?" he asked.

She regarded him.

"I'm thinking of asking Missy to stay on," he said. "You know, when Sable is—when Sable—" He looked at the girl as if she might have a better idea how to finish his sentence.

"When Sable dies," he said.

She slid off her stool. "I'm going to find my mom," she said, and he listened to her make her way down the hallway.

. . .

So Kayla felt the pressure of a deadline without any sense of what she was supposed to be achieving before it arrived. Two days had become a day and she had done nothing. But what was she supposed to be doing? Should she have told Henry about Shaw's plan? Should she have asked Henry for money? Should she have driven away?

She found Sable swinging on the porch swing with her eyes closed. She joined her. Sable opened her eyes. They swung together, pumping their legs, hanging on to the seat.

Kayla said, "Do you remember how we used to swing hard enough to hit the wall?"

"No," Sable said, smiling.

The next morning she still hadn't heard from Shaw. What had he meant by two days? He'd wait until dark and break in sporting night-vision goggles? She called and left a voice mail. *It's me*, she said. *Don't come.* And then she ran out of ideas.

Saturday Sable was on the high stool at the kitchen counter ripping open Splenda packets and pouring them out.

Kayla had quit trying to get her to stop and instead was making fried matzo. Sable had taught her as an eight-year-old how to cook it. Now Sable's contribution was to ask every ten seconds what time it was. Kayla told her it was almost time for breakfast. She felt herself growing impatient with the conversation. She was not competent to conduct it. It seemed designed to make her incompetence clear.

Henry was in the bedroom with Missy. Clare came into the kitchen and stood next to her mother, her shoulders doing their thing.

"What?" Kayla asked, trying to keep the not-again out of her voice.

"Henry says he wants to play carnival with Missy," Clare said.

"I don't know what that means," Kayla answered, adjusting the electric burner.

Sable ripped open another packet, poured it onto the back of her hand, and licked it up like a teenager doing tequila shots.

"He says she sits on his face and he guesses her weight. He says they're getting married."

Kayla put her forehead on the counter and stayed there. She rolled her head against the Formica. She missed Sable.

"Maybe you didn't hear right," she finally said to her daughter.

Clare said she wanted to go home.

Kayla straightened up, turned off the burner, and dished some matzo onto a plastic plate for Sable. She told Clare to stay put. She wiped her hands on her shorts and left the kitchen.

"I still want to go home," Clare called.

The bedroom door was closed. Kayla stood in front of it listening to the voices and the rustling.

As a kid, she had sometimes snuck out of her own house in the middle of the night to visit their bedroom. It was carpeted. Its bathroom night-light glowed yellow. She would stand there, letting her eyes adjust, and would watch the two of them sleeping, almost always curled around each other. Then she'd lie on the rug by the foot of their bed. They'd find her in the morning, and Henry would say, *Well, what have we here?* and Sable would usher her into their bed, still warm from their bodies, and go make her breakfast.

The first time she'd brought Shaw to meet them, they all had watched TV in there. Sable and Henry on the bed, and Shaw and Kayla on the floor with the corduroy armchair pillows Sable loved and Henry was always trying to get rid of. Shaw had made a fuss about the pillows and Sable had pushed at Henry's shoulder, triumphant, and for once Kayla had warmed with pride.

Later in the guest bedroom, Shaw moving inside of her, she'd asked how he'd known to compliment the pillows. Had she told him about them and forgotten? He'd told her it wasn't hard to make people happy; you just had to pay attention. And then he'd taken her hips and brought her against him again and again, making her come so hard she couldn't stop crying out.

In the morning Sable made them breakfast, poured them coffee, and asked how they'd slept, and then when Shaw left the room, turned to Kayla and told her it had been a mistake to let them sleep in the same room. The heat of shame had seeped through Kayla's chest and she'd said, sounding like a child, "You *like* him."

"Not that much," Sable said, swiping the counter with a sponge. "And that's not really the point, is it?" She stopped and Kayla could feel her care like a hand on her shoulder. "*You* don't like him," she said. "At least not enough." She added that she didn't have to be Kayla's mother to know that. And Kayla had answered that it was none of her business, since Sable *wasn't* her mother, was she? And the look that had put on Sable's face—that was one of many moments Kayla was never going to get a chance to fix.

When she opened the door Henry was in the bathroom naked from the waist down and Missy was kneeling by his feet, holding diapers for him to step into.

They didn't notice her.

Maybe what was going on was kindness; maybe it was love. What did she know?

She backed out of the room and closed the door; Clare was in the hallway behind her. Kayla told her Henry was fine.

Clare stood there looking at her. "Nothing you do helps," she said. She wasn't angry or sad, and Kayla steadied herself against the wall until her daughter walked back to the kitchen.

Shaw called at three that morning. Kayla was on the porch swing. Even at that hour, the air was like the insides of mouths. Florida sounds in Florida plants. The phone lit and buzzed in her hand like an insect.

"Thinking of me?" he asked. His voice sounded as if he were the one in a house full of people.

She felt as if she hadn't slept in weeks, strung out past limp to something like calm. "Where are you?" she said. He'd said he call when he was a few hours away.

Down the block, a set of headlights blinked on and off.

"I never learn," she said.

"What?" he asked.

"Trouble is always closer than you think," she said.

With his lights off, she could no longer see his truck. "Poor you," he said.

Clare had put herself to bed after dinner. When Kayla had checked on her, she'd pretended to be asleep.

"Is the door open?" he asked.

He had said this would happen, and here it was, happening. She answered yes, as if one thing would not lead to another.

Henry wasn't sleeping either. He coughed lightly and she hung up without saying good-bye.

"How's 'The Amazing Shaw'?" he asked, lowering himself into the swing next to her.

"What?" she said. Whenever she was getting ready to lie, she said *what?* first. "That was my girlfriend."

He smiled and called her Miss Glass. It was a name Sable had given her years ago. A way to let the girl know that they were paying attention.

Her eyes filled up and she closed them, leaning her head back. She told him everything. Shaw, Clare's school, the rent, the pregnant girlfriend, the painting. What Shaw wanted and how he wanted to get it.

Henry listened as if listening to reports of flooding in another country. He remembered that first time Shaw and Kayla had come to visit. He had overheard Sable tell Kayla she shouldn't have let them share a bedroom. He had turned to find Shaw standing behind him. Shaw had stood there and then he'd left.

Kayla was looking at him. She wanted to know what to do. She wanted him to fix everything.

He was tired. If Shaw wanted the painting, let him have it. What difference did it make? He stood and put his hand on her head. "What do you want me to tell you?" he said. "You know you can't be with this guy."

"So what do I do?" she asked.

"You're a grown-up," he said. "You figure it out."

She was crying harder now.

"I know you can," he added, because that's what Sable would've said.

She stood outside Henry and Sable's room to hear if he had fallen asleep. She went into Clare's room. Three night-lights were on. The fan made a low hum. She picked up Clare's owl sweatshirt and hung it on the back of a chair.

Clare's book was open across her chest. Kayla marked the page with a postcard they had picked up at the barbecue place and set the book on the nightstand. She bent over her daughter, put her nose to her hairline, and, her heart steeled against itself, breathed in.

Clare opened her eyes.

Kayla put her hand on her daughter's forehead and told her to go back to sleep, everything was fine. Clare kept looking at her. She took in the handbag over one shoulder, the backpack over the other. Her expression made clear that if what was happening was what she thought was happening, things might never be fine.

Help her, Kayla told herself. And then she thought that she had nothing to offer anyone. And this couldn't be the last time they would see each other. Her plan was to get away from where she'd been and from the person she'd become. Maybe Shaw would track her down, maybe he wouldn't. But what Shaw did or didn't do probably wasn't the point. She pressed her hand to Clare's chest and watched it rise and fall. *One, two, three. Magic*, she thought. Then she left.

At dawn Henry lay awake in bed. Hours earlier, he'd heard Kayla in the hall and the back door opening and closing, but he hadn't had the energy to investigate. Morning would arrive soon enough.

Their bedroom was as it always had been. The Amish rocker, the tennis rackets, the painting. He tried to concentrate on Kayla and her problems but he couldn't. He touched Sable's cheek and pretended she had a different illness and that this was their last night together.

They'd spend it in their bed. They'd fit their bodies together. He'd put his nose behind her ear. He'd hold her. They'd talk. She would come back. He'd be there to meet her.

She was still asleep. She looked like he remembered.

At a party, he had once heard someone wonder aloud what she was doing with him. It was a mystery, the other person had answered, and they had laughed.

The door opened to a small figure in shadow. "Mom's gone," Clare told him.

Of course she was, he thought.

Sable woke. She looked at the girl and turned back the covers. "Come in," she said.

Clare stood there, her shoulders moving up and down. "She's not coming back," she finally said.

"No," Sable told her. She sounded kind. Still, he said to the girl, "What does she know? Of course she'll be back. Until then, you'll be here."

It all seemed to make a certain sense to him, but in the dim light he could feel their wariness with each other. And who could blame them? Who knew what else was coming and how it would arrive? It was their job to bear up under its weight. Whatever it was, they'd be there to meet it.

"I remember you," Sable told her. "Come in," she said again, and she patted the space between them.

RESCUE

MORE THAN ONE OF THE TOWN RESIDENTS SAID THAT THE dog had stayed with Brenda Leroy until the ambulance arrived, that Pete Geary, who called 911, found the dog sitting on her chest, that Scott Hernandez, the first response officer, had to lift the dog off her, and that tugging on the leash had yielded only resistance. In retellings, this was a part of the story that got furrowed brows and hands to chests, yet some felt the detail to be implausible. After all, no one knew how much time had passed between her being hit and being discovered when Pete was driving home from his shift half an hour early so as to make the tip-off of his daughter's basketball game at the high school. It had been 6:30 pm on the Tuesday before Thanksgiving in this New England college town. The night was clear.

She had, apparently, been walking her dog, that Australian shepherd mix she had rescued against most of her friends' advice five years earlier. Her life, they had pointed out, was already a house of cards: one boy, nineteen, who she had to agree came with his own brand of parental challenges; a double mortgage on a house that had once been an actual chicken coop, bought at the height of the market; her health problems—diabetes and chronic back pain—which had meant one job after another over the last two decades. *You* have dogs, she'd countered when her friends had argued against her getting one. Amy Price had answered, "But *we* have help." Brenda knew *help* meant *husbands*, which Brenda did not have, had never had, and, though she was only forty-two, believed she would never have. She had thanked them for their advice and returned to the shelter the next day to sign the papers.

The car, the police department concluded based on two rivets found at the scene, was a late-model Honda. Some suggested this investigation might be beyond the crack capabilities of the local police force. More than a few residents, owners of late-model CR-Vs or Accords, scanned their brains for where they'd been Tuesday evening. Could they have hit somebody and not known it? they asked themselves before dismissing the possibility. Lisa Miller called her husband as soon as she heard. "Are you in the Odyssey?" she asked. "Were you driving down Tipton Lane at five or six?" Fred Miller said what he always said when faced with his wife's mild, usually harmless, hysterics: The big picture, please. Paint the big picture.

When she was done repeating what she'd heard from Sarah Hughes, who had heard from Abigail Bronkowski, who had a police scanner and whose father was a volunteer fireman, Fred Miller took a breath and asked if his wife was really suggesting that her husband of twenty-two years might've hit a woman with his car, left her in the road, and kept driving.

Lisa wondered if he might've thought it was a pothole or a branch.

"A branch?" he said. He told her he was hanging up now and would see her at home, and she sat with the phone to her ear long after he was off, defensive and grim about the way her anxieties were dismissed in their long and otherwise happy marriage.

Scott Hernandez had held the dog's leash while the paramedics stabilized Brenda's back and neck and loaded her into the ambulance. After they'd driven away, the dog had whined quietly and licked at Scott's hand. He was the shape and size of an Australian shepherd, with the long, layered fur, but had the blocky head of a Lab. Scott would've said he didn't like dogs much, but this was a belief borne more from childhood disappointments than actual sentiment. He'd had an anxious mother and a father ill-equipped to deal with those anxieties. His mother had resisted the children's desires for a dog, and his father had gone along. What would happen when the dog died or got sick? She could tell them what would happen: they'd be miserable, and she couldn't stand that. Scott and his sister had appealed to their father; he had regarded them sadly, but shrugged, conceding without an argument, and Scott had learned the small sad ways that marriage could eat away at a person.

So he had not expected the pleasure he felt at the dog's warm tongue against his palm. He headed up the road to notify Brenda's boy, who, he knew from his wife, a friend of Brenda's from aerobics classes at the Y, was home for the holiday. Jesse was twenty-four; he had lived with his mother, unable to bring himself to leave her to her own devices, until that October, when he'd moved to a town an hour away. He'd been gone less than a month.

By then, it still wasn't yet seven but had been dark for hours. The street was quiet, garage doors lowered for the duration. A few houses already sported Christmas lights. Most would be put up over the Thanksgiving weekend. It was a neighborhood of ranch houses and Colonials. There was more than one Children at Play sign. Basketball hoops over garage doors, pitching nets in front yards. Driveways were short and blacktopped. In the spring, touch-me-not impatiens would be the flower of choice around the bases of mailbox posts. Most of the husbands and wives on the block had grown up in town. Scott had known almost all of them since he was a boy.

The dog's tags jingled. "Nearly home," Scott said. He could see Brenda's house up ahead. To his wife and their mutual friends, he often expressed sympathy for her. A difficult situation, he would say. Caught some rough luck. Stuck between a rock and a hard place. But a part of him believed her situation to be more her fault than not, and therefore deserving of pity more than compassion.

Any number of them had been dealt a crap hand; it was what you did with it that made you who you were. It would take him months to get the images of her in the road out of his head, but he had to admit that he had not been surprised that it was her lying there.

He was not looking forward to ringing her bell. He stopped and the dog stopped with him, expectant and optimistic. He patted the shepherd's head and offered his hand again as if it held something the animal had always wanted.

Alex Ripton called home from the ambulance. He'd been an EMT with the Village Ambulance Service for six months and the others still gave him grief about how often he called his wife. He was unfazed by their teasing. She's my best friend, he told them. Hearing her voice is the best part of my day. They'd laugh loudly, and Alex would smile and continue to say the things he felt.

He'd been married for nine months to the only girl he'd ever dated. This would be their first Thanksgiving as a married couple, and they were hosting both sets of parents and all their siblings. He'd sat behind her in ninth-grade English and had fallen in love with the back of her head. When he'd told his boss that detail, his boss had stared at him and then asked what the hell that even meant. Alex had just shrugged and told him that if he didn't know, he couldn't help him.

He wasn't going to make it home in time for dinner after all, he said from the bench seat in the speeding ambulance. He watched his partner record Brenda Leroy's stats. They had to go to Central with this one. He wasn't supposed to share any details, but none of the paramedics paid attention to that rule, so he told her what he knew.

Jane Ripton texted her book club, and that was the way most of the town found out, twelve women armed with cell phones and information. Amy Price was one of those women, though she texted no one but her husband. Jesse would need help, she wrote, and she got to Brenda's minutes after Scott. Through the picture window at the front of the house, she could see him and Jesse standing in the living room. She didn't ring the bell; no one ever did. She knocked twice, businesslike and usual, and walked right in.

Over the next few days the town talked of almost nothing else. The local papers covered the story, telling residents almost nothing they didn't already know. The state police were involved. They had interviewed, fruitlessly, all the residents of Tipton Lane more than once. Brenda was in a coma and on life support. And when the papers used the phrase "neurologically devastated," many repeated it as if they had thought of it themselves.

Only Carol Li, who shared a driveway with her neighbors, Bert and Penny Misko, knew that the front fender of the Miskos' car, a late-model Honda CR-V, had, at least from her kitchen window in the early morning light three days after the accident, looked both damaged and freshly washed. She couldn't remember if it had been in the driveway the night of the accident or the day afterward, and if it had, she couldn't remember if it had been damaged in any way. So when she'd told the two officers who'd interviewed her that she knew nothing, she had not felt herself to be lying.

Carol Li was a Chinese lesbian who had moved here less than two years ago from Manhattan. She'd been hired as an assistant VP at the college, where until recently Bert Misko had worked as a locksmith. Her yard sported raised garden beds filled with organic radishes and kale. Theirs featured a decorative wishing well and campaign signs for Republican candidates who didn't stand a chance in a town like this. The Miskos liked Carol's chickens. They reminded Bert of the ones his father, a Czech immigrant, had kept. Recently, Carol had been finding Bert in her backyard, sitting on a three-legged stool next to her coop, watching them. Penny had been embarrassed, telling her husband of fifty-eight years that Carol didn't want an old fool sitting in her yard, but Carol had assured them both it was fine; he wasn't hurting anyone.

Carol thought Penny looked like the lifelong drinker she was rumored to be and felt sorry for Bert. Based on the recyclables, Penny's drink of choice seemed to be gin, and based on what Carol could hear through open windows in the summertime, Penny was a mean drunk, spilling over with resentments and grudges. As far as Carol could tell, Bert never left his wife to rage away on her own, never quit the house until she calmed down, and never retreated behind a closed door, but his own voice was always too quiet for Carol to hear. Once, Carol had looked out her kitchen window and seen Penny sitting on her back stoop, a martini in one hand, a cigarette in the other, a woman worn out by the gap between what she'd hoped for and what she'd gotten. Carol had recognized the exhaustion of keeping yourself protected from what the world threw at you. And this might have been the other reason she hadn't, at first, told the police what she had seen.

But then she had. The town claimed to be shocked by the arrests, but most confided that they'd always known Penny Misko would end up doing something like this. She'd always been a liar and a drunk; it was not hard to imagine that she could leave a neighbor in the road not twenty feet from her front door, could listen to the ambulance arrive from the comfort and darkness of her own home, could convince her husband to lie not once, but three times to the police, and could claim, even after having been caught, her innocence. She'd most likely been drunk. Didn't she have those previous two DUIs? Poor Bert had always been cowed by her.

The more compassionate suggested that maybe she hadn't known she'd hit someone, but they'd been dismissed. The car's windshield had been replaced! The police who'd retrieved it from the body shop said the damage was "consistent with something large striking it." Something like Brenda Leroy's head. The Miskos had left her in the street, and they'd sat there at their kitchen table listening to the ambulance come and go, and they'd lied, lied, and lied again. And Brenda was their neighbor. She'd known them her whole life. Penny had worked with Brenda's mother at the sleeping bag factory. Penny Misko was a terrible person. Not guilty? they said. Please.

Jesse Leroy had spent the better part of his childhood tending to a mother who refused to tend to herself. He'd wake to find her on the kitchen floor, in diabetic shock. Her back would go out, and he'd carry her to her bed or the sofa, help her eat, retrieve things she'd dropped. Some years she'd spent more time in the hospital than out. Friends would put him up to keep him out of foster care. He'd move from house to house, trying to be invisible, gratitude and rage filling his insides at these homes with their two parents and squabbling siblings, their full refrigerators and well-made beds. He could not yet understand that the picture those families presented to him might not have been complete, that rescuing him might have allowed them to keep their own fault lines at bay.

So he felt his whole life had been like the last several weeks: sitting in a plastic scoop chair by his mother's bed. Other people came and went. A lawyer produced papers Jesse hadn't remembered existed, a health care proxy, a living will, a power of attorney. An estranged aunt, a distant cousin, doctors whose specialties he could never keep straight. The same friends who had taken him in. Some brought food or hope, walked the dog or tendered advice. Especially Amy Price. Every time Jesse managed to take a break from the hospital and drive home for a few hours, it seemed Amy had been there. The house had been vacuumed, the garbage had been taken out, lasagna was in the oven, the porch light was on. Jesse liked her, always had, so he couldn't say why he could barely bring himself to say hello, why he couldn't offer thanks or gratitude.

He and his mother had always been a planet unto themselves, so when one of the doctors, apparently the neurologist, began to speak to him about removing his mother from life support, Jesse's instinct, like that of a stubborn horse, was to set his feet and resist.

The doctor spoke across her in her hospital bed, and it seemed so wrong. Hadn't the nurses been telling him that she could hear him, that he should read to her, talk to her? Didn't it seem wrong to be talking about this as if she weren't lying between them, as if she were already dead? But he had been humiliated by people like this doctor—teachers or principals, managers or store owners—his whole life, and he'd been working to still his rage in the face of them, and so he said nothing as the doctor talked about her lack of improvement, her lack of brain activity, about the very, very clear unlikelihood of her ever coming out of this.

What Jesse said was that he would think about it. What he didn't tell the doctor was that he and his mother had had an argument that Tuesday before Thanksgiving, and to end it she had grabbed the leash and said she was going to walk the dog; they would talk when she got back. So, no, Jesse thought, he would not be removing his mother from life support. That was something he could not do.

Carol Li found Bert Misko in her garage a few days after the Miskos' arraignment. She'd seen the newspaper photo of the couple standing in court, looking familiar and unrecognizable at the same time. The trial was set for April. They'd been released on bail.

She hadn't seen either of them since the arrests. The police had told her the source of the tip about their car would be confidential, but even Carol knew how this town worked. Yet Bert seemed pleased to see her.

She didn't know what to say. She was sorry? *Was* she sorry?

He smiled at her.

"I've been thinking about you guys," she finally said. It was true.

He nodded. "I know," he said. "We've been thinking about you, too."

It was a strange conversation. They regarded each other for a moment, and then he said he had to get to work; there was a lot to be done. He headed across the yard to his front door.

Jesse had not meant to get as upset with his mother as he had that Tuesday evening. Over the years, they had developed a kind of parallel play, like an old married couple, and this time it had been the usual resentment and anger at her way of saying one thing and indicating its opposite. Have your own life, she was always saying. Never leave me, she was always making clear. That Tuesday it had been her supposed enthusiasm over his new job and new apartment. She was so glad, she kept saying, that he had finally gone out on his own. She'd lit a cigarette and was blowing it out the back door, which she'd cracked open a couple of inches. The cold air crisped the kitchen. He was sitting at the small Formica table that Amy Price had given them when she had married and gotten a new one. The dog was at his feet.

"Why don't you just smoke in here?" he said, though he knew why she didn't. She wanted to believe she didn't smoke at all, and a house that smelled like cigarettes made that harder.

"I'm not finishing it," she said, stabbing it out against the frame and flicking it into the yard.

"That's the fourth one you haven't finished," he said. He didn't know why he said the things he did. Or maybe he did. It had been hard in the new town, at the new job, in the new apartment. It had been a month, but he still got lost making deliveries; his boss still yelled at him, wanting to know if he had any brain at all. The friend he was staying with was a high school friend who had recently graduated from college and was already making sounds about Jesse finding a place of his own. Jesse had thought he was moving toward something, but the gap between the world and him just seemed to be getting wider.

She opened a jar of olives and ate a few standing by the fridge. "Well," she finally said, "I'm glad you're moving on." She put the jar back in the fridge. "I was beginning to think I'd be taking care of you the rest of my life."

And Jesse had known she was baiting him, and that his leaving had been hard on her. He knew she was lonely.

But none of what he knew had kept him from saying what he'd said: that it didn't matter where he lived, that he'd be taking care of her until the day she died.

So when he eventually gave permission for her to be removed from life support, and against all odds she kept breathing on her own, but showed no other improvement, he figured that was about exactly what he deserved.

That Tuesday before Thanksgiving, Bert had been in his reading chair in the front room when Penny got home from teaching her four o'clock Senior Aquacise class at the Y. Recently, she'd felt little waves of relief every time she came home to discover him safe and sound. She knew she shouldn't leave him alone, but she couldn't afford at-home care, and a nursing home was not an option. So what was she supposed to do? Sit and stare at him all day long?

She knew she needed to take him to the doctor; she'd made an appointment weeks earlier but had canceled it. She didn't need a doctor to tell her what she already knew: her husband was losing his mind. Dementia, Alzheimer's, it didn't matter what they labeled it. She'd gone through this with both of her parents. She knew what was coming.

She told him she was going to take a bath and change, and then they'd get moving on dinner. Since he'd started acting not quite himself, she'd found herself narrating what they were about to do one or two steps before they did it, as if supplying him a script could keep him in the play. Maybe it was the warmth of the bath, or the dim quiet of the house. Maybe she had exerted herself in class more than usual; maybe it was the martini she sipped while bathing. Maybe the last few months with Bert had taken more out of her than she'd realized, but she closed her eyes and sank to her chin in the hot water. When she woke, the water was cool, it was past eight, and the house was still.

Their car was missing, as were Bert's keys. Why hadn't she hidden them? His shoes were under the mudroom bench. His coat was on the hook in the front hall, his wallet in the pocket. He was out somewhere in his slippers, she kept thinking, even as she understood this was not the biggest part of the problem.

After she had checked the house and the yard and the few streets nearest to them, she could think of nothing to do but wait. She had no one to call. She had avoided most socializing and had covered for his confusions when she had to. Their siblings had all passed, their nieces and nephews scattered far afield. If the police or a neighbor brought him back, she would tell them he was on a new medication, temporarily disoriented. If he found his own way home, she would not scold him. They had no children, which felt now like it always had: blessing and curse. She understood she would not have been an ideal mother. She understood she had not been an ideal wife. But when he finally pulled into the driveway at four in the morning, unable to explain where he'd been or how he'd gotten home, but so, so happy to see her, she had understood that wherever he was going, she was going with him.

She warmed his feet, and got him a cup of hot milk, and put him to bed with a heating pad and an extra blanket, and he reached out to hold her hand with his. He was agitated. She didn't know, he said, what he'd been through. The suffering had been enormous, he said. One day he would tell her all about it. He was afraid he had lost her. And then he was calm, insisting that she was too good for the likes of him, and she told him he was a fool and went downstairs to turn off the porch light.

And there was the car, in the driveway, where it was supposed to be, but there was the bumper and the windshield, and whatever relief she'd felt at his safe return slipped away. One end of the bumper was folded into itself. The windshield looked like a giant had struck it. It was cold and still dark. Carol's shades were drawn. Penny went inside. She stood, leaning over the computer. When she found what there was to find, a fist closed around her heart and she sank to her knees, because, ideal or not, for fifty-eight years she had been Bert Misko's wife, and she did not know how to be anything else.

The dog went everywhere with her: If she quit one room in the house for another, he got up and followed. If she was working in the yard, he patrolled the perimeter. He was well trained enough to go without a leash or a collar, but she always used both and the dog resented neither.

He was not a dog who held a grudge. His first situation had been unpleasant, but he had survived, and this one was better. He was grateful for where he'd ended up, refusing to dwell on where he'd been, and he sensed this was something that they had in common. What're you gonna do? she often said out loud to herself. He understood the meaning if not the words.

And he knew the car; it had passed them thousands of times. The man in it was unthreatening. It smelled of fuel and gravel, rubber and pine needles. He did not see it hit her, but he felt her pitch away from him, the leash yanking at his neck. The car never slowed, its smells disappearing away from where she lay. And this was not how she stayed in her bed or on her couch. This was different.

He sniffed her face. Metal and paint, blood and hair. He whined and barked once. The street was empty.

Lives were being lived all around them. He settled like a sandbag across her chest. It rose and fell beneath him. *Stay*, he thought. *She understands*, he thought, the woman in the road, the woman who had saved him.

ACKNOWLEDGMENTS

These stories cover over thirty years of writing. A lot of people are responsible for making them better. I, alone, am responsible for all their remaining inadequacies. Here is what I'm sure is a woefully incomplete list of the people to whom I owe big gratitude.

For teaching: Steven Millhauser, Gordon Lish, Rosellen Brown, Jim Robison, Mary Robison, Daniel Stern, and Richard Howard.

For editing: C. Michael Curtis, Willard Spiegelman, Betsy Sussler, Andrea Barrett and Ladette Randolph, Amy Hempel and Frederick Barthelme, Linda Swanson-Davies and Susan Burmeister-Brown, Maris Finn, Gregory Jordan, Cheston Knapp, and Hannah Tinti.

For agenting and more: Eric Simonoff.

For crucial support along the way: Andrea Barrett, Sandra Leong, Katherine Longstreth, Ann Mooney, Marsha Recknagel, Karen Russell, Gary Zebrun.

For crucial support in the final stretch: everyone at the extraordinary Tin House Books, but especially, Rob Spillman, Meg Storey, and Tony Perez.

For the family I was born into: Yungmei Tang, Sidney Glazier, Leonard and Zelda Glazer, Amy Glazer, and Mitch Glazer.

For the family I made: Aidan Shepard, Emmett Shepard, and Lucy Shepard.

For all of the above and way more than even he knows (and as anyone will tell you, he knows a whole lot): my husband, Jim Shepard.

THESE STORIES APPEARED PREVIOUSLY IN THE
FOLLOWING PUBLICATIONS:

"Fire Horse" appeared as "Mainland," *Southwest Review* and "Incognito with My Brother," *Bomb*

"Popular Girls," the *Atlantic*

"Jerks," *Mississippi Review*

"Magic with Animals" appeared as "The Palace of Happiness," *Columbia*

"Don't Know Where, Don't Know When," *Tin House*

"Girls Only," *One Story*

"Light as a Feather," *Ploughshares*

"The Mothers," *SB Nation*

"A Fine Life" appeared as "In My Country," *Glimmer Train*

"Kiss Me Someone" appeared as "There Be Monsters," *Tin House*

"Rescue," *Tin House*

KAREN SHEPARD is a Chinese American born and raised in New York City. She is the author of four novels: *An Empire of Women*, *The Bad Boy's Wife*, *Don't I Know You?*, and *The Celestials*. Her short fiction has been published in the *Atlantic*, *Tin House*, and *Ploughshares*, among others. Her nonfiction has appeared in *More*, *Self*, *USA Today*, and the *Boston Globe*, among others. She teaches writing and literature at Williams College in Williamstown, Massachusetts, where she lives with her husband, writer Jim Shepard, and their three children.